THE PARADOX

By Kathy Keller

Kathy Keller
Leesburg, Virginia
www.KathyKeller.com

Publisher's Note: This is a work of fiction. Names, characters, places, and incidents are a product of the author's imagination. Locales and public names are sometimes used for atmospheric purposes. Any resemblance to actual people, living or dead, or to businesses, companies, events, institutions, or locales is completely coincidental.

The Paradox/ Kathy Keller -- 1st ed.
ISBN 978-1-7370503-7-7

It is far better to grasp the universe as it really is than to persist in delusion however satisfying and reassuring.
—Carl Sagan

It seems that information and discovery isn't information and discovery without the type of 'proof' that the human race requires.
—Arjun Walia

CONTENTS

CHAPTER ONE

A RANDOM DISCOVERY

A sudden burst of intense energy snapped the sun's magnetic field. Fiery explosions tore across the surface of the sun, hurling clouds of charged particles—filled with magnetic field lines—into the exosphere.

In Boulder Colorado, scientists at NOAA's Space Weather Prediction Center monitored the cyclical solar storm through a bank of computers that recorded information on the size, solar wind speed and direction from specialized telescopes and satellites.

The division director approached a scientist studying the latest data. "Is the CMA still on course, Cheryl?"

The scientist nodded. "Yes, sir. The corona mass ejection will hit Earth with a glancing blow. The size and strength are low. It won't make a noticeable impact."

"Good, that's how we like it. Post it on NASA's website for the science crowd."

An hour later, the scientist was scanning readings from the magnetometers and plasma instruments; confusion rippled across his brow. "Cheryl, check out the coronagraph imagery from the CCOR again."

Cheryl looked at the data. She frowned, rubbed her eyes and checked it again. Alarm flooded her face.

"Sherman, get the director!" she shouted.

Across the country, an elderly woman suddenly gripped the arms of her wheelchair. She wheeled herself over to the window and gazed up at the cloud-laden sky. Nothing appeared out of the ordinary, but the dark foreboding continued to grip her, and a chill ran through her frail body.

In northern Virginia, a slight, middle-aged man walked through the security measures in the lobby of a corporate building.

"Calling it a night, Dr. Hamill? This is early for you," remarked the security guard as he searched the scientist's electronic devices.

Hamill nodded. "Not as young as I used to be, Joe."

The guard laughed. "They say 50 is the new 40, but I sure ain't feelin' it. You're all clear. See you tomorrow."

"As sure as taxes and death," replied the scientist.

Hamill picked up his computer and cell phone and left the innocuous building that bore no name and was hidden behind a screen of trees and manicured bushes.

When he arrived home to his fourth-floor high-rise, he fed the tabby cat, turned on the television, and went about preparing dinner.

The breaking news chime suddenly sounded, and an anchorman came on screen.

"The National Oceanic and Atmospheric Administration's Space Weather Prediction Center has issued a warning that a coronal mass ejection will hit earth in 48 hours, triggering a major geomagnetic storm that will affect satellites and wireless communication systems."

Hamill stopped what he was doing and turned to watch the newscast.

"All aircraft will be grounded, and officials worry that it may cause extensive damage to the power grids. They are advising that people be prepared for blackouts across much of the Northern Hemisphere for several days.

"Earlier data had indicated that the corona mass ejection would have minor impact. Scientists are baffled by the sudden dramatic change. According to a NOAA spokesman, this has never happened before. A geomagnetic storm of this magnitude has not been seen since the Carrigan event in 1859—"

Hamill snapped off the television and was still for a long moment. His features tensed as the NOAA spokesman's statement—*This has never happened before*—reverberated in his mind.

He picked up his cell phone and called a contact at the Space Weather Prediction Center.

The scientist was reluctant to answer his questions. "The director is on the hot seat, Amos. We've been told not to talk to anyone until we figure this out. Why are you so interested?"

"I have a theory," replied Hamill.

There was a long pause on the other end of the phone.

"Glad someone does. It was the damnedest thing. We'll never get this egg off our face…. What do you need?"

"The readouts and coronagraphs for the last 48 hours," said Hamill.

There was another long pause.

"All right, but if you discover something, I get the credit, Amos."

"If I'm right, you won't want the credit," responded Hamill.

* * * * *

Fairfield, Pennsylvania

Kip Stevens drove the remote two-lane country road from Addison to Fairfield. Habit didn't dictate it. He liked to feel connected to the outside world. Radio and cell phone reception in this area at the foot of the Allegheny Mountains was spotty at best. And he liked the conveniences of gas stations and fast-food restaurants.

But today, it was the most convenient route, and the negatives were moot points. Everything was closed. Satellites and electricity had been down for hours since the geomagnetic storm had hit, and no one was predicting when normalcy would return.

Twilight was falling. The road was deserted, making the situation seem even more surreal. It would appear people were heeding the advice of the mayor and the governor to stay at home. If things didn't get back to normal soon, thought Kip, he would have to type up his story on a manual typewriter. Did any still exist? he wondered.

As he rounded the bend, the headlights of the car caught something ahead several feet off the side of the road. It looked like a pile of clothes in the grass. Kip slowed down as he approached the area, peering closely through the window. Suddenly, he jammed on the breaks, jumped out of the car, and ran over to the site. A man lay crumpled on the ground.

Kip bent down and rolled him over. He was a young man and looked as though he'd been in a fight. He had cuts and bruises on his face and one eye was swollen shut. He didn't move or speak. Blood covered much of his shirt-front, and Stevens saw that the man had been shot. He felt for a pulse. It was thready. Just then, the man moaned and his eyes flickered open.

"What's your name?" asked Kip. "What happened to you?"

The man stared up at him blankly, and Kip saw that he was in shock.

"I'll take you to the hospital," he said.

He carefully hoisted the man to his feet and half carried him to the car.

CHAPTER TWO

A MYSTERY PATIENT

Kip sat slumped in a chair in the dimly lit waiting room of Fairfield Memorial Hospital waiting for word from the doctor, when police detective Hank Gillespie ambled in wearing his usual frown.

He heaved a sigh of annoyance when he saw Kip. "I should have known. Why aren't you at home like everyone else?"

Kip looked up at the short, stout detective and bit back a grin. The detective's ode to fashion was a mismatched hairpiece that topped his head like a dust bunny begging to be liberated by a stiff wind and a suit too long in the coat, too short in the trousers—all of which served to undercut his gruff demeanor.

"Just doing my job, Gillespie. Neither snow nor rain nor heat nor gloom of night—"

"I don't think that was meant to apply to pain-in-the-ass reporters," retorted the detective.

"Where have you been? I thought the donut shop was closed," joked Kip.

"Funny, Stevens. The comms are down at the station. The hospital just sent someone over to notify us. Can't get a cup of coffee anywhere," the detective griped. "What's the word on this guy's condition?"

"I don't know. He's probably still in surgery," replied Kip. "The doctor hasn't come out yet."

Gillespie pulled out a notebook and pen. "Give me the details."

"I was out covering the effects of the storm on the area and was on my way home by way of the back road," explained Kip. "I found the poor guy lying off the side of the road about 15 miles from Fairfield and brought him to the hospital. That's it."

"Name?"

"He wasn't conscious long enough to say," said Kip.

The doctor walked into the waiting room then, still in his scrubs.

Kip stood up. "What's the word, Doc?"

Gillespie glared at the reporter. "I'm asking the questions here." He turned to the doctor. "What's the word, Doc?"

The doctor passed a hand wearily across his face. "We removed the bullet. The first 24 hours are always touch and go, but barring any complications, the young man should make a full recovery. He was lucky. If Kip hadn't come along when he did, we might be having this conversation in the morgue."

"What about a description?" asked Gillespie.

"I'd put his height at about 5'10", medium build, brown hair, mustache with that close-cropped goatee young men like to sport these days," replied the doctor.

"Age?" quizzed Gillespie.

The doctor thought for a moment. "Mid-twenties, I'd say."

"Name?"

"He never regained consciousness and was rushed into surgery soon after Kip brought him in. No I.D. was found on him."

The detective turned to Kip. "Stevens, did you see a wallet on the ground where you found him?"

Kip shook his head. "But I wasn't looking. I was a little distracted at the time."

Detective Gillespie snapped his notebook shut. "I'll get a man out there to search the area. When can I talk to this guy, Doctor?"

"Not until morning, Hank. He's heavily sedated."

"I'll need that bullet and his clothes. We don't know what this fellow might have been into."

The doctor nodded. "I'll have the nurse get them for you."

CHAPTER THREE

NO MEMORY

The next morning, the detective returned to the hospital and found the doctor at the nurse's station updating a file.

"Is he awake, Doc?"

The doctor looked up. "Didn't expect to see you this early, Hank. Yeah, he's awake, but I don't think he's going to be of much help to you."

"Why not?" asked Kip, coming up behind the detective.

Gillespie grimaced and turned to him. "What are you doing here?"

"I saved the guy's life. I want to know how he's doing," said Kip.

The detective snorted. "Who are you kidding? You just want a story." He turned back to the doctor. "Go on, Doc. You were sayin'?"

"The young man appears to have amnesia," reported the doctor. "He doesn't remember anything—not his name or where he's from."

Gillespie eyed the doctor with skepticism. "Do you believe him? Pretending amnesia is a good way to avoid answering questions if you were involved in a criminal act."

The doctor shrugged. "He was pretty disoriented, but then again he was still sedated."

"Which room is he in?"

"I'll take you there," said the doctor. "Go easy."

As Kip started to follow, Gillespie stopped and turned to him. "Where do you think you're going? This is police business."

"C'mon, Gillespie. If he has amnesia, an article about him on the front page might bring someone out with information."

"Kip is right," said the doctor.

Gillespie hesitated. "Don't get in the way. And if I tell you something is off the record, Stevens, it's off the record," he warned with the wag of his pen.

As the three men filed into the room, the stranger turned his head. His jaw was swollen, one eye was blackened, and an ugly bruise had spread across his cheek.

"This is Detective Gillespie," said the doctor. "He needs to ask you a few questions. And this is Kip Stevens, a reporter for the *Fairfield Gazette*. It was Mr. Stevens who found you."

"The doc says you don't remember much. What do you remember?" asked the detective.

The man's eyes darted around the room. "This isn't right," he whispered anxiously, his voice hoarse. "Nothing is right...these machines...I don't belong here." He started to thrash. "I have to leave."

The doctor put a retraining hand on the patient's shoulder. "Calm down now. You've just had surgery."

"Who beat and shot you?" asked Gillespie.

The man just looked at him. "I shouldn't be here."

"Where should you be?" quizzed the detective.

The man started to drifted off.

"That's enough for now," said the doctor. "He needs rest. I'll let you know if he remembers something."

The men walked into the hall.

"There's more to this guy's story," said Gillespie.

"Gee, do you think?" remarked Kip.

Gillespie glared at him. "You know what I mean. I think the amnesia is a convenient excuse."

"If it is, the guy is pretty convincing," said Kip.

CHAPTER FOUR

MRS. THURSTON

Stevens strode into the police station three days later and greeted the guys with a box of donuts.

"Is Gillespie in?" he asked the duty clerk.

The clerk nodded. "He's at his desk—and he ain't in a good mood."

"He's never in a good mood," interjected a patrolman, snagging a donut.

Kip laughed. "Don't let him hear you say that."

He climbed the stairs to the detective division on the second floor. "Hey, Gillespie, any word yet on the John Doe fingerprints?"

The detective looked up from his desk, a pained expression on his face. "Geez, Stevens, don't you have other assignments?"

The reporter grinned. "Not as interesting as this one. Did you find anything?"

"Give me a chance already. We're still backed up from the solar storm." Gillespie stood up to put a file in the cabinet. "From what we can tell, your guy isn't in any databases. We circulated his picture to police departments around the country, but nothing has come back."

"If his fingerprints aren't in the system, then he hasn't committed a crime," conjectured Kip.

"That we know of," reiterated Gillespie.

"He wasn't in the military or worked any kind of job requiring a security clearance?" asked Kip.

The detective shook his head. "We got zip." He sneezed and put a hand to his hairpiece to make sure it was still in place.

Kip's lips twitched with amusement. "What about John's clothes? Did you check the labels?"

Gillespie pursed his lips in annoyance. "Who's the detective here, Stevens? Of course, I checked. Peg said the clothes are vintage…from a New York store that went out of business in 1934. She figured he probably bought them in one of those retro stores…maybe was in the theater or something."

"The playhouses around here are closed for the season," said Kip.

"Then maybe the guy is just offbeat. Hell, Peg wears those crazy clothes from the hippie era." Gillespie nodded toward a middle-aged woman sitting across the room. "Why don't you ask her?"

Kip regarded the woman. She looked like one of a dozen others one might encounter on the street—plain dressed, gray hair, menopausal weight around the waist—not one who would garner particular notice one way or the other.

"Who is she?" he asked.

"Supposed to be a psychic," replied Gillespie.

"A psychic!" exclaimed Kip. "What's she doing here?"

"You know the five-year-old kid that went missing two days ago?"

Kip nodded. "The family was on a camping trip, and he wandered off."

"The parents insisted on bringing her in," said Gillespie.

"No shit. Is she for real?"

Gillespie shrugged. "They found the kid a half hour ago—right where she said he'd be. She just touched the kid's sweater the search team found and told them they were looking in the wrong place…. I thought you would have been all over this story, Stevens."

"Anderson caught the assignment," said Kip.

"John Doe still isn't remembering anything?"

Kip shook his head. "Not as far as I know. The hospital isn't allowing visitors. The doctor brought in a psychiatrist, and they're running more tests."

He glanced over at the woman again. "What's her name…the psychic?"

"Mrs. Thurston," replied Gillespie.

"Do you still have John's clothes?" asked Kip.

"Talk to Peg. Now get out of my hair!"

Kip ran up the steps to the lab on the third floor, got what he needed, and rushed back down to the detectives' squad room.

The psychic was just leaving.

"Mrs. Thurston," he called out.

The woman stopped and turned. "Do you need another statement, detective?"

"No. I'm not with the police," said Kip. "I'm a reporter for the *Fairfield Gazette*—Kip Stevens. I heard how you were responsible for finding the little boy. Have you always had this ability?"

"Yes. My great grandmother, grandmother and mother all carried the gift," she replied. "I regret to say my grandmother and mother considered it more of an affliction and chose to hide it rather than to put it to good use. Those days were not as forgiving of people who were 'different.' But I don't give interviews, Mr. Stevens."

"I'm not asking for an interview, Mrs. Thurston. I have another kind of request."

"How can I help you?"

Kip told her about finding John Doe injured along the side of the road and of his amnesia, careful not to give away too much detail.

He showed her some suspenders. "John was wearing these when I found him. I was hoping you would be able to tell me something that might help to identify who he is."

When she hesitated, Kip assured her that he would pay her for her service.

"Mr. Stevens, I don't do this for the money," she said tersely. "I'm happy to help if I can. But I don't perform to prove myself to skeptics."

"Point taken, Mrs. Thurston, and I'm sorry if I offended you. This is not a test. I really am at my wit's end, and the police have no leads."

"And I'm your last resource."

Kip gave her a rueful smile. "Afraid so."

"That's all right, Mr. Stevens. I'm used to it. I realize that I may be feeding your skepticism, but I must warn you. This is not a gift that comes at my beckoning."

Kip nodded. "I understand."

Mrs. Thurston took the suspenders and threaded the straps slowly through her fingers, focusing her gaze on a distant point.

"I'm seeing mathematical formulas," she said. "I keep getting the name Tessa—no Tesla."

"It used to be one of the hottest cars on the market," said Kip.

Mrs. Thurston shook her head. "No, this is a man."

"John's name?"

"No, but he has something to do with that name," replied the psychic. "This man Tesla was a physicist…long time ago." The psychic looked at Kip confused. "How old is John?"

"I don't know exactly. The doctor thinks he's in his mid-twenties."

"Mr. Stevens, I'm seeing a man over a century old and hearing the name Slaterville."

Kip was startled for a moment before remembering that John was wearing vintage clothes when he was found. She was probably getting her wavelengths—or whatever they were—crossed, he thought.

"I'm sorry. That's all I'm seeing," said Mrs. Thurston, handing the suspenders back to Kip. "I hope it helps." She held out her card. "If I can be of more help, please call me."

"Thanks. I'll let you know," replied Kip, his tone noncommittal.

Mrs. Thurston smiled. "That's what all skeptics say when they don't get the answers they are seeking. But you know, eventually, they do get them. Be patient, Mr. Stevens. The universe works in mysterious ways."

She started to leave, then stopped and turned back to Kip. "You need to go to Slaterville, Mr. Stevens. I don't know for what reason, but my guide is most insistent that you go."

CHAPTER FIVE

JOGGING A MEMORY

It was a few more days before Kip was permitted to see John.

On his way to the hospital, he stopped by a bookstore and bought a book about Nikola Tesla. He was eager to see John's reaction to it—and to test the psychic's abilities.

Kip signed in at the desk and walked down the hall to John's room. A woman wearing a white doctor's coat was just leaving it. She looked young, and Kip figured her to be a physician's assistant checking on John's recovery.

She wore little makeup—a touch of blush and lip color. Her auburn hair was loosely gathered on top her head, and she wore the black "librarian" glasses to give her an extra air of authority—or so Kip guessed. Either way a nice touch, he thought.

"You are here to see," she looked down at her iPad, "patient number 203?" she asked.

"I call him John…for John Doe," said Kip.

She looked up at him with a humorless expression. "Yes, I get that. I'm Dr. Porter, the psychiatrist assigned to 'John's' case."

Kip blinked in surprise. Except for the glasses, nothing else was according to type. "You're a shrink?"

"Psychiatrist," she corrected him coolly.

"Sorry. Usually shrinks—I mean psychiatrists—don't look like you," replied Kip.

At the raise of her brow, he instantly knew he was in trouble.

"What I mean to say is that you don't look old enough," he quickly amended.

"I get that a lot," she responded, annoyed. "I can assure you that I have all the necessary credentials."

"I think I should stop talking now," said Kip.

"Yes, that might be advisable." Dr. Porter fixed him with appraising hazel green eyes framed by long dark lashes. "You must be Mr. Stevens."

It was a flat statement of fact, and Kip wondered how to interpret that. If she had heard he was a bonehead, he had proved her point.

"Ah—how is the patient today?" he asked, redirecting the conversation.

"Physically, his injuries are healing," she replied. "Mentally, he's having dreams that disturb him. It's common as the memory struggles to come back. Fragments of a person's life usually come in flashes or dreams with no order," she went on to explain. "I'm having 'John' moved to the psych unit so I can observe him more closely."

Her eyes went to the book that Kip carried. "Is that for him?"

Kip nodded. "I thought it might jog his memory. The way he was freaking out over technology, I didn't think he was ready to surf the net on a computer yet."

"It's best not to press him," said Dr. Porter. "He's having great difficulty accepting the fact that this is the 21st century. He seems to think this is 1903. I'm trying ease him into the present to avoid a psychotic break."

Kip's eyes widened, and he stopped short of uttering an expletive. "That's strange," he murmured.

"What is?" quizzed Dr. Porter.

Kip hesitated. "John was wearing clothes from that era when I found him."

She looked at him in surprise. "He was wearing period clothes?"

"Maybe that's why he's confused," said Kip.

Dr. Porter was silent for a moment, her expression troubled. "May I see the book?"

Kip handed it to her.

She looked at it and frowned. "Nikola Tesla—he was a physicist in the last century. Why did you choose this subject?"

Kip swallowed hard. After the inglorious first impression he had made with her, he wasn't about to say that he was following the lead of a psychic.

"Uh, coincidence," he replied. "I heard that John had an interest in science."

She took off her glasses and slipped them into the breast pocket of her coat. "I don't think it's a good idea. It will feed his delusions, Mr. Stevens."

"Doctor, if he's so obsessed with the past, the topic might help him to remember who he really is," suggested Kip. "It's worth a shot."

She considered the matter and handed the book back to him. "Please be careful what you say to him, Mr. Stevens."

As she started down the hall, he called out to her. "Call me Kip."

Dr. Porter glanced over her shoulder at him and continued on her way. He wasn't sure that was a good sign.

Kip pondered this new development. It was going to harden Gillespie's suspicions about John all the more. Hell, he didn't know what to make of it himself.

When Kip entered the room, John was sitting in a chair.

"Well, you are looking better," he said. "I'm Kip Stevens."

The man looked up at him, showing little emotion. "Yes, I remember. You're the one who found me. Thank you for helping me."

Kip nodded. "Anytime. Have you recalled anything?"

John shook his head. "Only that I know this isn't where I am supposed to be. The doctor said that sometimes people don't want to remember because they fear what the truth may be. Detective Gillespie seems to think I was involved in some criminal activity. What do you think, Mr. Stevens?"

Kip hesitated. "I can't say with any certainty one way or the other until I know more facts. But I've been a reporter for many years, and my instincts tell me that you're not a criminal."

John sighed. "Well, I suppose that is something. Thank you, Mr. Stevens."

"Call me Kip. I brought you a book. Maybe it will help you to remember something."

John took the book and looked at it. "Nikola Tesla," he murmured. "I think I know him." He scanned through several more pages, then stopped on one and stared at it. "Slaterville…that name sounds familiar."

Kip was taken aback. The psychic had mentioned Slaterville. "It's a town not far from here. Maybe you live there," he suggested.

John puckered his brow as he struggled to remember. "No…I was there for another reason—with Mr. Tesla." He looked up at Kip. "You must contact Mr. Tesla. He can tell you who I am."

Kip caught his breath. Mindful of Dr. Porter's warning, he casually retrieved the book from John and decided to let her tell him that Tesla had died in 1943.

SLATERVILLE

Ted Dittmore was not a tall man, but his large, solid frame gave heft to a sense of authority. The thatch of silver hair and bifocals were his only concessions to advancing years, golf his only vice.

As the longtime Managing Editor of the *Fairfield Gazette,* he doggedly held to three principles: journalistic integrity, provable facts, and economy. Thus, he met Kip's request with little enthusiasm. It violated the last two tenets.

"Why do you want to go to Slaterville? And why do you need four days?" quizzed the editor. "It's an hour away."

"I have a lead I need to follow up," said Kip.

The editor's eyes narrowed as he scrutinized his reporter. "If this is about that fellow you found, I thought I told you to drop it."

"He's certain he was in Slaterville, Chief. It doesn't hurt to check it out." Kip thought better of not mentioning the psychic.

"Look, I let you run his picture and the story," argued Dittmore. "No one has come forward with information. I have other assignments for you to work on. You already missed one deadline.... Your guy probably got rolled in a card game...or a drug deal went bad."

Kip scoffed. "You sound like the police. Anything they can't explain, they pin on drugs. For your information, no drugs were found in John's system, and there was no sign of drug use."

"John? You got a name?" questioned the editor with more interest.

"No. I call him John…you know, for John Doe?"

"Oh, well, it doesn't mean that he wasn't dealing drugs and trespassed on someone else's turf," insisted Dittmore.

Kip snorted. "Come on, Ted, the guy was dressed in period clothes when I found him. He's probably an actor or something."

A thought suddenly flashed in the editor's mind. "Wait a minute. You said he was dressed in period clothes?"

Kip nodded.

Dittmore rummaged through the papers on his desk and came up with a page of copy. "This came across my desk a few days ago to run in the paper. Slaterville is celebrating Founders' Day. Townspeople are dressing up like in the old days to give tours and lectures. Your guy is probably one of these re-enactors."

Kip took the copy and read through it. "All the more reason for me to go to Slaterville. Someone must know him."

The editor sighed heavily. "A guy was mugged. He temporarily lost his memory. It happens every day somewhere. What's the story here, Kip?"

Kip shook his head. "I'm not sure yet," he replied ruminatively. "I just have this feeling."

Dittmore tapped his fingers on the desk as he considered the matter. He glanced over at Kip. There was no denying the guy had a nose for stories.

"You can have three days," said Dittmore, "on your dime."

"Gee, you're generous to a fault, Ted. Wasn't it you who said that pulling on a small thread can lead to the unraveling of a big story?"

"I don't see a story here big enough to justify making it a covered assignment, Stevens. If you find something to change my mind, I'll okay picking up your expenses."

Dittmore paused. "This is a small-town paper, Kip, not the *Philadelphia Inquirer,* and Fairfield isn't your usual crime and corruption beat. If you can't get used to that…"

Kip nodded. "Message received."

* * * * *

Slaterville was located 65 miles northwest of Fairfield and once a thriving lumber town until the timber played out in the 1920s. Now, it was a quaint tourist destination on the register of historic towns, thanks to an anonymous benefactor as the story went.

The tourists were out in force for the fall colors, and the celebration was an added draw. Townspeople wore clothes like the ones John had been found wearing, boosting Kip's confidence of discovering the man's identity.

As Kip maneuvered his way through the congestion of cars, pedestrians, and horse-drawn carriages to a large historic home, now a bed and breakfast, he counted himself lucky to have gotten a last-minute reservation. He checked into the B&B and showed the clerk an image of John on his iPhone. She didn't recognize him.

Kip drove to the library. Inside the old gothic building, he found his way to the research department.

The librarian was friendly and dressed in period clothes as well. "Are you a visitor in town for the celebration?" she asked.

"Actually, I'm here on another matter, but it would seem that I have come at the right time," replied Kip.

She reached for a pamphlet on the counter. "This is a schedule of events you might find interesting. At two o'clock, 'Alexander Graham Bell' is demonstrating his telephone at the museum. And you won't want to miss 'Mr. Tesla's' amazing demonstration of electricity at the theater on the square at four o'clock. Both men were visitors to the city, you know."

"I knew that Mr. Tesla was here in the early 1900s," said Kip.

"October 1903," the woman proudly informed him.

Kip took out his cell phone and pulled up John's photo. "Do you know this man?"

The librarian studied the image. "Sorry, I don't recognize him. Was he in an accident? He looks pretty banged up."

"He was found injured on the side of the road near Fairfield. He can't remember his name or where he's from, and he was wearing period clothes. When I heard about your Founders' Day Celebration, I thought he might be a participant," explained Kip. "The name Tesla seems to hold special meaning for him."

"The poor man. Ask Mrs. Rappaport the town historian," suggested the librarian. "She knows everyone in town and did all the hiring for the re-enactments. Her office is in the old Slater Homestead. Is there anything else I can help you with?"

"Yes. I would like to see back issues for the last two weeks of the *Evening Star* please," replied Kip.

The librarian brought him the issues, and Kip sat down and looked through them, searching for any mention of an occurrence that could be linked to John—a mugging, a shooting, a drug bust. He found nothing. Kip looked at his watch. He still had two hours until the Tesla demonstration.

He left the library and walked around town taking pictures of it in the meantime. At four o'clock, he made his way across the square along with a sizable crowd to the restored Victorian theater.

The minute Kip walked into the building, he felt transported back in time. Mosaic floors, globe wall sconces, and huge gilded mirrors decorated the lobby. Cream-colored columns supported a balcony and box seats, easily accessed by a grand wrought iron and brass staircase.

As Kip moved to the main floor seats with the other tourists, he shared their awe at the opulence of the architectural details. Acanthus leaves and scrollwork in gold leaf adorned the proscenium arch and framed the Baroque ceiling mural. Crystal chandeliers gave off a soft glow of light. Pastel colors of peach and green enhanced lavish plasterwork against cream white walls and gold fixtures. Together with the plush crimson velvet that draped the stage and covered the seats, the effect was jaw-dropping, especially to one accustomed to the minimalist style of the 21st century.

Kip found a seat with a clear view. When everyone was seated, the actor strode onto stage followed by an assistant. John had to have been acting as an assistant in some of these performances, he thought with increased optimism.

The man portraying Tesla bore a striking resemblance to the scientist and copied his manner and showmanship right down to the white coat and tails.

As accustomed to technology as people of this day and age were, the actor still managed to amaze with displays of electric current arcing from Tesla coils. People gasped when jags of lightning leaped across the stage and volts of electricity seemingly ran through the actor's body. Kip could imagine the effect it must have had on an audience over 100 years ago.

At the end of the performance, Kip approached the actor and the assistant and congratulated them. He showed them the picture of John, certain they would recognize him as a fellow actor. When neither could identify him, Kip was surprised. The pieces fit so neatly together. There couldn't possibly be any other explanation.

"Are you sure?" pressed Kip.

The Tesla actor nodded. "Sam and I are the only ones who play these parts. I've never seen this man before."

"Neither have I," said Sam.

Kip left the theater perplexed and disappointed. He caught dinner at a tourist spot and went back to his hotel.

The next morning, he was up early and stopped by police headquarters to make further inquiries.

"Oh yeah, we got a general inquiry from Detective Gillespie with the Fairfield Police," said the duty officer. "We checked missing persons and incident reports but couldn't find anything on this John Doe."

"Did you notice anyone acting strange a couple of weeks ago?" asked Kip.

The cop laughed. "Sure. There was a solar storm and a full moon."

Kip smiled. "I mean stranger than usual. Did you have an incident report two weeks ago of a shooting that was maybe linked to a mugging or a drug deal?"

"Nope. Just the usual small-town stuff—domestic quarrels, a couple of drunks in a fight, traffic violations. There hasn't been a shooting in Slaterville in two years," replied the duty officer. "You might ask Mrs. Rappaport over at the Historical Society about your guy. She knows everyone and everything that goes on in this town."

Kip drove to the old Slater mansion. It was located on the far side of the historical district in an area that had been the most fashionable part of town in its day. And like all the other tourist spots in town, parking was at a premium.

Finally, finding a space a block away, he walked to the house and hurried up the steps of the Queen Anne style mansion to once again, be swept into the world of the Victorian.

The parlor, dining room, and drawing room were typical of the period with textured drapes, ornately carved woods, heavy upholstered furniture, and wallpaper stamped with geometric and floral designs. The rooms were roped off to the public, allowing tourists a view from only the foyer and hall.

A pleasant, older woman in period dress came from a back room to greet him. "Welcome to the Slater home and the Historical Society," she said. "Our tour begins in 30 minutes. You're welcome to wait in our café, which is located in the carriage house."

"Thank you. Are you Mrs. Rappaport?" asked Kip.

"I am," she replied.

Kip took out his cell phone and held up the photo of John. "I am told that you know everyone in this town, and I was wondering if you might know the identity of this man?"

The woman put on her glasses that hung from a chain around her neck and looked at the picture. "My, my, what happened to him?"

"He was mugged and has amnesia," said Kip. "Do you know him?"

"He does look familiar," she said ruminatively. "I know I've seen him before, but I can't seem to remember where."

Just then, a group of visitors walked in.

"Oh, please excuse me while I take care of these people," she said. "Why don't you have a look in our exhibition room just down the hall? Maybe I'll remember something in the meantime."

"I'll do that. Thank you," replied Kip, feeling more encouraged.

He walked into the room that had been Jefferson Slater's office, according to the plaque. Two long rows of exhibit cases displayed personal items of the Slaters, as well as some artifacts of other pioneers of the day—the Marshalls, the Trowbridges, and the Claymores.

As Kip's eye roved over the pictures of events, people, and landscapes lining the walls, his gaze came to rest on a large oval portrait of a young woman. The plaque identified her as Elizabeth Slater, daughter of founding father Jefferson Slater. The date was 1904.

She looked to be in her early twenties, and she had the classic 'Gibson Girl' beauty with blue eyes, light brown hair dressed in the popular Pompadour style, and soft flawless features. But there was such a palpable air of sadness about her Kip had difficulty taking his gaze off her. He took out his iPhone and snapped a picture of the oil portrait, wondering what her story was.

He came to another picture of her in an earlier photograph. She and an attractive young woman impishly mugged for the camera, suggesting that Elizabeth Slater had a playful personality.

As Kip regarded other photographs of her, he realized that all the ones in which Elizabeth appeared happy were taken in or before 1903. Something had occurred then that took the light from her life, he deduced.

He came then to a photo of her with a young man. The man sat on a chair stiff and erect and looked sternly into the camera. All in all, he was an attractive man, but there was something cold and exacting about him. Elizabeth stood stiffly beside him with a hand on his shoulder, projecting the same sadness that Kip had seen in her portrait.

"She was beautiful, wasn't she?" commented Mrs. Rappaport.

Kip was startled from his musings. He hadn't heard her come into the room.

"Yes, she was very pretty," he replied. "Did something happen in 1903, Mrs. Rappaport? Judging from the photographs, there appears to be a marked change in her after that point. She looks so unhappy in these later photographs."

"The later photographs are more formal. It was the style not to smile in formal pictures," explained the historian. "The portrait of her over there was her wedding portrait. This photograph was her wedding picture with her husband Thomas Marshall."

"What happened to her?" asked Kip.

"Well, we don't really know," admitted Mrs. Rappaport. "We have no record of her after 1907."

"There's no death notice or burial site for her?" questioned Kip.

The historian shook her head. "None that we could find."

"Isn't that unusual for a woman whose father was instrumental in the founding of the town?"

Mrs. Rappaport sighed. "Women lived in the shadows of their menfolk then. Unfortunately, history was not concerned with them unless they did something notable or notorious. There was some talk that she left town."

"You mean she left her husband," said Kip, reading between the lines. "Formality aside, it's obvious she wasn't happy in these later pictures."

"It was rumored that the marriage was not a happy one," admitted the historian. "Oh, I remembered where I saw the man in your photo."

She led Kip over to another wall of pictures and directed his attention to a press photo. The caption beneath it read: Nikola Tesla demonstrating the Tesla coil, October 14, 1903.

"Is that your man?" asked Mrs. Rappaport, pointing to the assistant standing to the side of the theater stage.

Kip looked at the man. His jaw dropped and his pulse quickened. The assistant was the spitting image of John. This man had to be John's great grandfather—or a close relation to him.

"Does this help you?" asked the historian.

"Mrs. Rappaport, I could kiss you." he told the astonished woman.

He snapped a picture of the press photo, left a generous donation and hurried out of the house.

After a quick lunch, he drove to the library and requested copies of the newspaper for the month of October 1903. The librarian brought them to him on microfiche.

Slowly, he scrolled through the daily editions until he found the notice for Tesla's lecture series and articles on the event. And there was the photo that he had seen in the Slater House. According to the newspaper, Tesla had remained in Slaterville for two weeks.

Kip came to more photographs of Tesla with the social elite taken at receptions and dinners. He recognized Jefferson Slater and Elizabeth Slater, Winston Marshall and his son Thomas, Julia Trowbridge with her new husband Lawrence, but there was no further mention of Tesla's assistant. He obviously hadn't ranked with the elites.

"Have you found what you're looking for?" the librarian asked.

"No, not really. Do you have copies of the newspaper for the rest of the year on microfiche?" asked Kip

"I'll check," she said.

Kip didn't know why he was bothering. Tesla and his assistant had undoubtedly returned to New York by this point. It was a waste of his limited time. He was trying to figure his next move when the librarian returned with another canister.

Kip stretched his back and flexed his fingers, then loaded the microfiche. He found it odd that the first paper to come up on the monitor was dated November 15, 1903. Issues for the first half of November were missing. But then anything could have happened back then—a fire, a flood. He scrolled through the first two pages and was about to move on to the next one when a notice buried at the bottom of the page caught his eye.

ITINERANTS TO BE TRIED IN DISAPPEARANCE OF TESLA ASSISTANT—Abner Cook and Billy Jenkins will be tried next week for the deplorable murder of Riley Harrington that occurred on November 1st. Mr. Harrington had accompanied the esteemed scientist Mr. Nikola Tesla to Slaterville on the 14th of October to assist with lectures and demonstrations of the Tesla coil. Mr. Tesla and Mr. Harrington departed two weeks later, but apparently, Mr. Harrington had seen fit to return for reasons unclear and ran afoul of the pernicious suspects. Mr. Tesla is reported to be quite grieved over the death of his assistant.

This was a big story for the time, especially for a small town. Yet, it was little more than a footnote inside the paper. Kip took out a pen and notebook from his bag and jotted a few notes.

He read through the next papers.

A Friday edition of the following week held another small notice that the men accused of killing Riley Harrington were sentenced to 10 years in the state penitentiary. The culprits refused to divulge the whereabouts of the body and, in the absence of one, were convicted of manslaughter in the commission of a robbery as circumstantial evidence was compelling enough to warrant it, read the article.

Kip searched through the rest of the papers for more information. But he found nothing more on the story. He sat back in his chair with questions.

He returned the microfiche to the librarian and headed back to the police station.

"Hey, did you find out who your man is?" the duty officer asked when Kip walked through the front door.

"Yes and no," said Kip. "Where would I get information about a shooting that occurred November 1, 1903? Two drifters were accused of killing a man named Riley Harrington."

"Did you try the newspaper? The library has most of the old editions on microfiche."

Kip nodded. "I just came from there. It appears there was very little coverage of the event."

"Well, if the case was closed, the files would have been sent to the courthouse to be warehoused after four or five years," the duty officer informed him.

"Thanks. I'll try there," said Kip.

"Won't do you much good," said an older officer in the room. "There was a fire at the courthouse in 1908. All the files from 1890 to 1908 were lost."

"Oh, yeah," recalled the duty officer. "I forgot about that."

Kip groaned. "There are no police records at all for 1903?"

The older cop shook his head. "Sorry. The only accounts would be newspaper accounts.... You might try talking to Herbert Whitley. His grandfather was a cop on the force about then. Herb's memory is pretty good. He might remember something."

CHAPTER SEVEN

MADDIE CLAYMORE

"I'm 92 years old," Herbert Whitley proudly announced as he led Kip into a dated living room. "I live on my own. The wife died five years ago."

He motioned Kip to an overstuffed chair and slowly lowered himself into a worn recliner. "My daughter wants me to move in with her, but I'm not budging. She always has grandkids running around. You say you're a reporter?"

"Yes," said Kip. "I'm looking for information on a shooting that occurred in 1903."

"That was well before my time, you know."

Kip smiled. "Yes, I know. But I understand that your grandfather was a policeman then. I wondered if he had talked about the case. A man named Riley Harrington was shot."

The elderly man drew his bushy white eyebrows together as he thought about it. "Can't say as I recollect mention of it."

"Riley Harrington was Nikola Tesla's assistant," explained Kip. "Did your grandfather tell you about the time that Nikola Tesla came to town to give a lecture in 1903?"

"Oh, sure," said Whitley. "Every school kid in Slaterville hears that story in ninth grade science. It was quite the thing." He chuckled. "Everyone thought Tesla had electrocuted himself. His suit was still smoking at the end of the demonstration. It was the talk of the town. I just saw in the paper there's a re-enactment of it for the Founders' Day Celebration. I'll have to take myself on over there and have a look see."

"I saw the show yesterday. It was quite impressive," said Kip. He took out a copy of the 1903 newspaper photo he had printed from his cell phone and pointed to John's likeness in the picture. "This is Riley Harrington."

Whitley picked up a magnifying glass from the side table and peered closely at the figure. "Oh, yeah, I remember now. Two drifters were accused of killing him in the grove."

"The newspaper account was sketchy, and all the court records were destroyed in a fire. Did your grandfather ever talk about the case?" asked Kip.

Whitley pursed his lips, thinking. "Once, my grandfather, my father, and I were sitting in the parlor listening to the war news, and it came across the radio that Tesla had died. Dad asked my grandfather about that case then."

Kip pulled out his notebook and pen from his jacket pocket. "What did your grandfather say about it?"

"Well sir, as I remember it, Grandfather said these fellows come tearing into town in a lather yelling about lightning bolts in the grove and the gates of hell opening up and swallowing Harrington."

Whitley laughed and slapped his knee. "The police saw they was liquored up, but they was so bug-eyed the police went to check it out."

"Did the police find anything?" pressed Kip.

"Just some scorched earth and a few burned trees they figured was from lightning…no sign of Harrington," replied Whitley.

He chuckled. "Grandfather said that was all it took for preachers to get people riled up about judgment day. You see, there had been a strange light in the sky for a couple of days—borealis they call it. People heard crackling in the air, the telegraph had gone down."

Kip looked at the elderly man in surprise. "There was a solar storm in 1903?"

"Don't know about that," said Whitley. "But people were nervous as hell, and after the rantings of those drifters, Grandfather said as how they was afraid to come out of their houses. Folks was pretty superstitious then…still are."

Kip scribbled notes in his version of shorthand.

"What happened to the drifters?" he asked.

Whitley ruminatively stroked his chin. "Grandfather said the story started to bring in reporters from the outside, and the town's bigwigs didn't like that," he recalled. "The judge held a bench trial closed to the public, sentenced the men to jail, and that was that."

Kip looked at him. "There was no body. No one questioned it?"

"Grandfather said the police found Harrington's coat with blood on it in the grove—and a gun that belonged to one of the drifters," replied Whitley. "I guess that was enough.

He leaned forward and gave Kip a meaningful look. "In those days, when Slater, Marshall and Trowbridge wanted something done, it was done, no questions asked."

"I'm well acquainted with the type this day and age," remarked Kip. "Why was Harrington in the grove that night? It's an isolated area."

Whitley shrugged. "Can't answer that. The drifters said they was hired to rough him up and send him packing."

"Who hired them?"

Whitley chuckled. "They claimed not to know. The police figured the drifters just picked Harrington as an easy mark and forced him to the grove to rob him."

Kip flipped the page on his notebook and continued jotting notes.

"Do you know if Harrington had a wife and a child?" he asked.

Whitley shook his head. "Can't say."

"Did those men ever confess to killing Harrington?" quizzed Kip.

"According to my grandfather, all they ever admitted to was rough-ing up the guy," replied the elderly man. "They said Harrington was hit with a stray bullet when they defended themselves against— what-ever it was."

"Did these men die in prison?" asked Kip.

"No, sir. Grandfather said new information come to light that showed the drifters didn't kill Harrington, and they was released."

Kip furrowed his brow in bewilderment. "So, did Harrington die that day or not?"

"I asked my grandfather the same question," said Whitley. "He didn't want to talk about it anymore. Never did say." The old man looked at Kip with curiosity. "With most of the old-timers gone now, the story has been forgotten. How did you come to hear of it?"

Kip told him that he had become intrigued about Riley Harrington when he came across the notice about the shooting in the *Evening Star*.

"When I went to the police department for more information, I was told the records were destroyed in a fire," he continued to explain. "One of the officers told me that your grandfather was on the force at the time and that you might be able to tell me more."

Whitley nodded, pleased with the referral. "You know, my father said that, as long as he could remember, my grandfather wouldn't go back to that grove. Even now, people are afraid to go in there."

"Why is that?" asked Kip.

"Well, over the years, there have been reports of animals acting strange. Some people claim that their pets have gone missing in the grove," replied Whitley. "It does give you the creeps some."

Kip underlined the word "grove" in his notes and flipped his note-book shut. "Thank you for your time, Mr. Whitley. You've been a big help."

He moved to leave, when another thought came to him. "Mr. Whit-ley, do you know anything about Elizabeth Slater? She seems to have disappeared from history in 1907. Mrs. Rappaport said it was rumored that she left town and was never heard from again. I gathered she had left her husband."

Whitley searched his memory again. "Yes, that was the story put around. But her carpetbag was found at the train station. Some people thought her husband had gotten wind of her leaving and did away with her, but nothing ever came of the investigation. My grandfather wouldn't talk about that case neither. The elites had ways of protecting their reputations, you know."

The old man rubbed his forehead, struggling to remember more. "I believe Thomas Marshall was in and out of a sanitarium after that and ended up committing suicide. You won't find that in the newspaper either…. Maddie Claymore might know more of the story. Her grandmother was a close friend of Elizabeth Slater."

Kip opened his notebook again and wrote down the name. "Where can I find Miss Claymore?"

"Maddie moved into the nursing home on Spruce Street. She's four years older than me." Whitley laughed. "She was a real looker in her day and a handful. She smoked and could drink any man under the table and, oh boy, did she break a lot of hearts. Made me wish I was older," he added with a wink.

"She and her grandmother and mother fancied themselves as some kind of—what do you call them—spiritualists," he continued. "The women in her family always were a little off beat. I suppose that's what made them so interesting."

Kip smiled, amused. "Thank you for your time, sir."

"Yeah, sure, anytime. If you're going to see Maddie, gotta warn ya she don't like reporters."

"Why is that?" asked Kip.

Whitley laughed. "She says they never get anythin' right but the gossip."

* * * * *

As Kip followed a nurse down the hall of the Greenview Manor nursing home the next morning, he wondered how fruitful this visit would be. He was depending upon a person's memories, not of her life but of her grandmother's. How lucid could the woman be at the age of 96—if she agreed to see him at all?

When the nurse knocked and opened the door, he was surprised to see a small, nicely furnished apartment. In a far corner of the living room, a slight figure sat in a wheelchair half turned toward a large picture window that looked out over a garden.

"Miss Maddie, you have a visitor," said the nurse. "He's a reporter from Fairfield."

"I don't have time for reporters," she responded curtly, continuing to stare out the window.

Kip could hear the contempt in her voice. Whitley was right. Apparently, she still hadn't forgiven reporters for past transgressions.

The nurse walked over to her and turned the chair around. "Now be nice, Miss Maddie. Slaterville is celebrating its 150th birthday this month. You are living history. Mr. Stevens wants to ask you some questions about past events."

Maddie gave a short laugh. "I've been called a lot of things in my day but never living history. Come over here, young man, so I can see you. My eyesight isn't what it used to be."

Kip moved closer.

A cloud of snow-white hair crowned her head and framed her face; thin pale skin exposed a network of fine blue lines; and despite what she said, her gaze was probably as clear and sharp as his, thought Kip. Her body might be frail, but he had no doubt that there was still a backbone of steel in there.

He introduced himself. "I'm Kip Stevens from the *Fairfield Gazette*. I would appreciate it if you could give me a few minutes of your time, Mrs. Claymore."

"A few minutes may be all the time that I have left," she shot back.

Kip smiled. "I'll try to be brief, Mrs. Claymore."

"Miss Claymore," she corrected him. "I never had a use for contrived conventions either."

"At least reporters rank with the institution of marriage," quipped Stevens. "I was afraid it might be lower—on the level of politicians."

She cracked a smile. "You have spunk, young man. I'll give you that. What kind of a name is Kip?"

"It's short for Kipling. My mother is an English Lit professor. One of her favorite authors is Rudyard Kipling."

The old woman nodded. "As long as there is good reason for it. I dislike these odd names with no more purpose than to be different. You may go now, Jan. I believe I can handle Mr. Stevens."

"It's not you I'm worried about," replied the nurse.

Miss Maddie snorted. "For heaven's sake, I'm not going to eat him, Jan. And Mr. Stevens strikes me as a man who can take care of himself."

"All right, but visiting hours are over in 30 minutes." The nurse looked at Kip. "If you need me, just yell," she said with a playful wink.

She left, and Maddie leveled her sights on Kip once again. "Sit down, Mr. Stevens," she commanded in a steadier voice.

Kip immediately did as she instructed. Even armed with Herbert Whitley's warning, he found her as intimidating as his ninth-grade history teacher.

"Please call me Kip," he said.

"I prefer to keep things formal," she replied. She fixed piercing blue eyes on him. "What do you want to know?"

Kip took out a small recorder from his pocket. "May I record you?"

Maddie snorted again. "If you must. I'm not a fan of electronics."

He clicked on the recorder and set it on a table.

"Interview with Miss Maddie Claymore, Greenview Manor Nursing Home." He looked at his watch and recorded the time and date.

"Miss Claymore, I understand that you are a lifelong resident of Slaterville," began Kip. "You have seen a lot of changes over the years. Your family has been quite socially prominent throughout the history of the town—"

"You are dancing, Mr. Stevens. Ask me what you really want to know."

The woman's insight and candor threw him off balance for a moment. "You are a very direct woman, Miss Claymore. I don't usually find that in people in my occupation."

"I have to be direct. At my age, Mr. Stevens, time is of the essence."

"If determination factors into longevity, I believe you underestimate the number of your remaining years, Miss Claymore."

Again, she allowed a faint smile. "You must have some Irish in you. How did you find your way here? Who sent you?"

"I was talking with Mr. Whitley about Slaterville in the early days, and he suggested that I talk with you," replied Kip.

Her eyes narrowed with suspicion. "Why? That old goat seems to know everything. Why would he send you to me?"

"He said that you could tell me more about Elizabeth Slater, since Miss Slater and your grandmother were close friends."

Miss Maddie peered closer at Kip. "Why do you want to know about Elizabeth Slater?"

"I was over at the Slater House and saw pictures of her. I could see a marked change in her in photos taken after 1903. I was curious to know what might have transpired to have such an effect on her," explained Kip.

Kip immediately felt a wall go up.

"Why should that interest you?" quizzed the old woman.

Kip shrugged. "I suppose it's the reporter in me, but mysteries intrigue me."

"You think there's a mystery here, Mr. Stevens?"

"Well, Miss Slater did disappear in 1907 and not even Mrs. Rappaport, who appears to take her position as town historian very seriously, can say what had happened to her," replied Kip. "I'd say that qualifies."

The old woman sat silent for a moment, her gaze riveted on Kip as though she was divining something about him.

"How old are you, Mr. Stevens?"

"Forty-two," he replied.

"A seasoned reporter, are you?"

"I like to think so," said Kip.

"Yet you are working for a small-town paper."

"It's a long story, Miss Claymore."

"Are you married, Mr. Stevens?"

"No—Miss Claymore, with all due respect, I'm here to interview you."

She smiled. "It's not comfortable opening your life to a stranger, is it?"

Kip was taken aback for a moment. When he saw what she was doing, he had to smile, too. "Point taken, Miss Claymore."

"Good. Now we can move on. Why are you here, Mr. Stevens?"

Kip furrowed his brow, confounded. "I told you. To find out about Elizabeth Slater," he replied, beginning to wonder about her mental state.

"No, why did you come to Slaterville?" she restated. "It wasn't to know about Elizabeth Slater."

"Why do you say that?" asked Kip.

"You only learned about her after you were here." Miss Claymore narrowed her eyes. "And you don't strike me as a man who has the time or patience for Founders' Day celebrations and old stories shaded by faulty memories and exaggerations. So, what is your real reason for coming to Slaterville, Mr. Stevens?"

Again, Kip was thrown off balance by her candor and perception. "You're right. I came here to follow up on a lead to another story," he confessed.

"What story?"

She was doing it again, flipping the script, he realized.

"I'll show you my cards if you show me yours," said Kip.

Maddy laughed. "It goes against my grain, but I like you, Mr. Stevens. Deal."

Kip told her about John Doe and of John's amnesia. "He thinks he's been to Slaterville. I came to see if anyone could identify him."

"And did anyone identify him?" she asked.

"Only Mrs. Rappaport and she thought him to be a man in a 1903 photo. I have to admit there is an uncanny likeness. I thought the man might be John's great grandfather."

Kip took out his cell phone and showed her the picture of John, then pulled up the assistant's image in the 1903 photo. "You can see how closely these two men resemble each other."

The old woman gasped. A look of such alarm contorted her features that Kip feared she might be having some kind of an attack.

"Miss Claymore, are you all right?" When she didn't answer, he jumped up and started for the door. "I'll call the nurse."

"No!" she exclaimed. "I'm fine. Please take your seat."

Kip wavered. She looked so pale. "Would you like some water?"

"No. Just sit."

Still hesitant, Kip sat down again.

"Did you find this man you call John dressed in clothes of that era?" she asked, a note of urgency in her tone.

Kip looked at her in surprise. "Yes. How did you know that?"

"Are you a religious person, Mr. Stevens?"

"No, not really," he replied.

"Good. Then it will be easier for you to learn."

"Learn what, Miss Claymore?"

"The truth, Mr. Stevens. Keep your eyes and ears open. Do not discount anything that doesn't fit into your perfect little world of logic and physics. And be prepared to straddle two worlds—the world of belief and the world of disbelief."

Kip didn't know what to make of this sudden turn of conversation.

Just then the nurse came in. "Visitor hours are over, Mr. Stevens."

"Please, just one more minute," said Kip. "Miss Claymore, do you know who John is?"

"He's Riley Harrington, of course," she replied, matter of fact.

"No, that is the man in the 1903 photo—Tesla's assistant."

"Yes…Riley Harrington."

The woman was obviously confused and, once again, Kip felt as though he had hit a wall. She had seemed so sharp at the start—to the point of setting him back on his heels a few times—before the conversation dissolved into nonsense, and he was hard pressed to hide his disappointment.

"I'm sorry, Mr. Stevens. You must leave now," said the nurse.

Kip nodded. "Thank you for your time, Miss Claymore."

She didn't answer, and Kip could see that her mind was elsewhere.

As he picked up his recorder, he heard her mumble: "He had to be a damn reporter."

Kip hung back, hoping she would say more. But she didn't, and he reluctantly followed the nurse from the room.

"Does Miss Claymore fade in and out like this often?" he asked as they walked into the hall.

"What do you mean, Mr. Stevens?"

"Lucid one minute, confused the next."

"Confused…Miss Maddie?" The nurse laughed. "She may be a bit eccentric, but that old girl is sharper than most people half her age."

"What do you mean by eccentric?" asked Kip.

The nurse laughed again. "She claims she can feel the Earth's vibrations."

CHAPTER EIGHT

MORE MYSTERIES

Kip left the nursing home annoyed with himself at being so easily drawn down the proverbial rabbit hole. He had thought himself too experienced for that. But the day hadn't been a total bust. He did have one thread to pull on.

When he got back to his room, he took out his computer and hooked it up to the internet. When he typed in the name Riley Harrington, nothing came up that matched with the age or information on the photo.

Kip thought for a moment. He had found in his research that Tesla had conducted most of his experiments at a New York lab in Manhattan. Kip quickly pulled up the census data on Ancestry.com for the year 1900 for the borough of Manhattan. Bingo. A Riley Harrington, occupation scientist, popped up. It had to be him, thought Kip with rising excitement.

To establish a timeline, Kip went on to search the 1910 census. There was no mention of Riley Harrington there or anywhere else in New York, New Jersey, or Pennsylvania. A check of the state censuses for 1905 for those states produced no further information either, and Kip had to conclude that Harrington had died in 1903, as reported, in spite of the questions that surrounded the account.

Given the dates, it was hard to see a connection between John Doe and Riley Harrington, but the resemblance between them was just too uncanny to ignore. Was it coincidence? Kip was not a strong believer of it.

He was trying to figure out his next move, when he noticed the recorder on the desk. He turned it on and listened to his interview with Maddie Claymore. The conversation had gone sideways, he noted, when he asked about Elizabeth Slater.

* * * * *

The next morning, Kip stopped by a florist for a bouquet of fall flowers and drove to the nursing home, trying to figure out how to convince Maddie to see him again.

"Mr. Stevens," greeted the receptionist. "Miss Maddie has been waiting for you."

Kip blinked in surprise. "She's been waiting for me?"

"All morning," replied the receptionist.

"O-o-kay. Then I best not keep her waiting," said Kip.

He walked down the hall to the apartment suite and tapped on her door.

"Come in, Mr. Stevens," commanded a frail voice.

He entered the room. "Good morning, Miss Claymore," he greeted, and handed her the bouquet.

"It's been a long time since a handsome, young man tried to bribe me with flowers," she quipped. She waved him to a chair. "Sit down."

"How did you know I would come back?" asked Kip.

She set aside the flowers. "You're a reporter. You have questions. Of course you would come back."

"You didn't show me your cards, Miss Claymore."

"I did, Mr. Stevens. You didn't know how to read them…. You asked me about Elizabeth Slater yesterday."

"And you didn't want to talk about her," said Kip. "Why?"

"There's an order to the story, Mr. Stevens."

"What story?"

The old woman smiled. "The story that you don't realize you are chasing."

Kip sighed. "I'm sorry, Miss Claymore, I don't have time for riddles."

"Perhaps this will help." She drew out a red, leather-bound book with the name Julia Trowbridge embossed on a cover worn smooth from decades of handling.

"It's my grandmother's diary," she said, handing it to him. "My grandmother passed it on to my mother and my mother on to me. I never married and had children. I've always wondered to whom I was destined to pass it. After you came to see me yesterday, I knew—it's you."

Kip wasn't sure how to respond to that. "Uh, Miss Claymore, I appreciate your willingness to entrust me with your grandmother's diary, but I came to Slaterville to find a clue to John Doe's identity," said Kip.

The lady cocked her head. "How good a reporter are you, Mr. Stevens?"

"Modesty aside, a good one," he responded.

"You're going to need to be. There's a larger story here, Mr. Stevens, than you can imagine and much of which I don't understand myself. But I can tell you with certainty that an imbalance has occurred in the universe, and now equilibrium must be restored before it's too late."

Kip stared at her. "I beg your pardon?"

"The universe is like a living, breathing entity, Mr. Stevens. It expands, it creates, it destroys, it restores, and it is mother to billions of worlds that, like children, can go astray. Right now, ours is one that needs to be brought back into balance, and I cannot impress upon you the urgency of it."

As Kip continued to stare at her, the old woman smiled. "I'm not crazy, young man."

"Sorry. I—you're pulling my leg, right?"

Maddie was silent for a moment. "Do you believe in random events or that some things happen for a reason, Mr. Stevens?"

"I never really thought about it," he replied.

"No one does until something happens that exceeds his or her realm of explanation. Do you think it was by accident that you found John or that you made your way to me?"

"I suppose people would say that it's coincidence," he responded.

"What do you say, Mr. Stevens?"

"I would call it luck," said Kip.

The old woman scoffed. "Another term for something people can't understand or explain."

"What do you call it?" questioned Kip.

"A process…the universe moving people around so that they are in the right place at the right time for a purpose that will be revealed to them when the universe is ready," she replied. "You, Mr. Stevens, are being moved into place."

Kip felt as though he was being drawn down another rabbit hole.

"You say there's a story, Miss Claymore. Why don't you tell me what it is, and let me take it from here?"

"I can't, Mr. Stevens. You wouldn't believe me. You must uncover the facts for yourself."

She pointed to the red book in his hands. "I've given you the key. The rest is up to you. Now, you must leave. You have much work to do. And you do not have long to do it."

Kip didn't argue. He was wasting his time here, he decided. This was his last day in Slaterville, and he had to make it count.

"Thank you for your time, Miss Claymore."

He stood up and walked to the door.

"Mr. Stevens," she called out, "everyone is led to the truth. But too often people don't choose to accept it. Instead, they substitute a truth of their own and create a world of illusion for themselves. Don't be one of those people. Much depends on you."

Kip walked out of the nursing home convinced that Maddie Claymore was delusional. She was an interesting woman but crazy. What had the nurse said—Maddie could feel the Earth's vibrations?

Kip glanced at the diary in his hand. He thrust the red book into his computer bag. Tomorrow, he'd return it to Miss Claymore on his way out of town.

He grabbed a quick lunch and drove to the library to do more research.

Kip found a quiet corner in the reference section and slipped off his jacket. He was fresh out of options and decided to approach the investigation of Riley Harrington from another perspective. He took out his computer to search the records of the state penitentiary from the year 1904.

Kip let out an expletive.

The librarian was passing by, and he flagged her down. "Miss, I can't get on the internet."

The librarian made a face and apologized. "I'm sorry, sir. I'm afraid the service is only as good as the phone company here. The internet goes down once or twice a month. A technician will be here soon."

Kip heaved a sigh of annoyance. His day kept getting better and better. He was putting the computer in his bag, preparing to leave, when he noticed the diary. Oh, why the hell not? He had nothing better to do at the moment.

He took out the book and opened it. The paper was yellow with age, the passages written in the neat, meticulous penmanship of the era. The first entry was January 3, 1903. *Dearest Diary, today I walked the riverbank...*

Kip settled back prepared to be bored with the silliness of a young woman's musings. To his surprise, succeeding entries were filled with wickedly funny observations and gossip as Julia Trowbridge poked fun at the indulgences of ego and wealth of the elites. She often quoted her dear friend Elizabeth, who seemed to share her views and a similar bent for witty satire.

Kip snorted. The elites haven't changed since then. He thumbed through the next several months filled with similar entries and stopped at a passage that caught his eye.

OCTOBER 14, 1903

Elizabeth and I attended a most interesting lecture and demonstration on the merits of something called alternating current. A scientist named Nikola Tesla conducted demonstrations to the town's great amazement. Elizabeth's interest, however, strayed beyond the event to Mr. Tesla's assistant and his to her. His name is Riley Harrington.

Kip eyes widened. Elizabeth Slater and Riley Harrington? That was unexpected, and he quickly paged to the next entry.

OCTOBER 15, 1903

Mr. Tesla is to remain in town for two weeks with his assistant Mr. Harrington. Elizabeth is quite giddy at the prospect. This does not bode well.

OCTOBER 20, 1903

Mr. Harrington asked Mr. Slater for permission to call on Elizabeth. Mr. Slater refused and was quite firm in his stance. He has bartered an agreement with Winston Marshall for Elizabeth to marry Mr. Marshall's son Thomas and wants no distractions to that end. Elizabeth is devastated. She dislikes Thomas and is hopeful of swaying her father. I fear her naïve. Oh, the price a woman pays for money and privilege.

OCTOBER 21, 1903

Elizabeth and Mr. Harrington have been exchanging notes with my assistance. She has asked me to help her arrange an assignation for tomorrow under the pretense of a shopping trip. I love Elizabeth as a sister and cannot deny her. Have I a hand in her doom?

OCTOBER 25, 1903

Last night, a reception was held in Mr. Tesla's honor. Mr. Harrington was not in attendance. Elizabeth suspects her father's hand in this.

OCTOBER 26, 1903

Mr. Slater keeps Elizabeth confined until Mr. Tesla and Mr. Harrington depart Slaterville. I have become her go-between with Mr. Harrington.

OCTOBER 27, 1903

Elizabeth and Mr. Harrington have laid plans to run off together. Mr. Harrington will pretend to leave with Mr. Tesla tomorrow but will return to take her away. Elizabeth pretends acquiescence so that her father relaxes his guard over her. I wring my hands in fear.

NOVEMBER 1, 1903

Elizabeth is quite nervous. Tonight Mr. Harrington returns. They are to meet in the grove.

Kip stopped. The grove—that's why Harrington had been there that night. He tucked it in his mind and resumed reading.

Elizabeth is a terrible liar and does not hide her emotions well. I fear her father will suspect something. There have been strange, beautiful lights in the sky bannering it in a spectrum of color that defies my poor attempts at description. Scientists call it a borealis. People think it an ill omen.

Was this the larger story that Maddie Claymore had hinted to him? wondered Kip. A story of star-crossed lovers? It wasn't his beat.

He shoved aside the diary and opened his computer to review his findings on John's identity. He had none—except this crazy resemblance to a man who had died over a hundred years ago with whom

John had no seeable connection…. But who was involved in a doomed relationship recounted in a diary that had been placed—no thrust—into his hands by an eccentric old woman who claimed the world was unbalanced.

Kip raked a hand through his hair and gave a mirthless laugh. He couldn't make this stuff up. He glanced sideways at the book. Elizabeth Slater and Julia Trowbridge called to him from its pages like sister sirens. Unable to help himself, he picked it up.

Pages were missing. The next passage began in the year 1905.

JUNE 15, 1905

It has been a year since Elizabeth was pressed into marrying Thomas Marshall. She is so miserable. He is such a cold fish. Although I am in an unhappy union of my own, my heart aches for her. She thinks about Mr. Harrington every day. Two men are imprisoned for his death, but, as long as there is no trace of his person, Elizabeth holds out hope that he is alive and will one day come for her. It is a hopeless dream. She bitterly blames her father for Mr. Harrington's disappearance.

Kip quickly skimmed through the next several months that dealt with the responsibilities of being the wife of a man of importance and a member of the elite, all which Julia found quite tedious.

He stopped at an entry announcing the death of Jefferson Slater March 10, 1906. "Elizabeth cries no tears for him—only for her lost love," Julia wrote.

Again, the journal came to an abrupt end until the following year.

OCTOBER 16, 1907

Elizabeth has inherited a sizable fortune in bearer bonds from her father. Thomas pressures her to give him power of attorney over them. She refuses. Each day, Elizabeth fears his temper more.

OCTOBER 28, 1907

*Thomas is desperate. He lost all his money in the Heinz brothers'
scheme and market collapse. Needs Elizabeth's money.*

NOVEMBER 1, 1907

*Elizabeth still refuses to sign over her bonds to Thomas. He threatens
to have her committed to the Mental Hospital.*

More pages had been ripped out. Why were so many pages missing
from the diary? wondered Kip.

There was one last entry.

DECEMBER 1, 1907

*Elizabeth is at peace and happy now. I shall no longer have the
comfort of my dearest friend by my side. I shed no tears. She is with
her love.*

Kip closed the diary, his mind churning. What was Julia Trowbridge saying? That Riley and Elizabeth had lived out their lives
together incognito? Or that they both had died—under mysterious circumstances?

CHAPTER NINE

NO LOGICAL EXPLANATION

Ericka Porter poked her head in the door of the medical director of the psychiatric unit of the hospital.

Taking note of the older woman's pixie haircut and petite, elfin-like features, she was moved to remark: "Does anyone ever tell you that you look like Judi Dench?"

Dr. Leanne Wolcott looked up from the computer on her desk and laughed, her blue eyes twinkling. "A younger version, I hope, but compliment accepted," she replied in a smoky voice. "If that's an attempt to pick my pocket, I have to warn you it's sewed shut."

"No, I'm here to pick your brain. Do you have a minute?"

The administrator took off her glasses. "Of course. Come in."

Ericka walked into the office and sat down.

"What's up? You look disturbed," noted Dr. Wolcott.

Ericka sighed. "Stumped would be more the word. You know the patient with amnesia that I have?"

Dr. Wolcott nodded. "You diagnosed him with dissociative amnesia."

"I thought he was exhibiting symptoms of repressed memories at first, but now I'm not so sure," said Ericka.

The director leaned back in her chair. "Why? What has changed for you?"

"He doesn't feel comfortable with his surroundings, Leanne."

"That shouldn't be surprising if he doesn't remember anything, Ericka."

Dr. Porter shook her head. "No, it's more than that. The technology upsets him. He can't relate to any of it, and this is compounding his confusion and frustration."

"Amnesia patients often have memory loss of past years," the director pointed out.

"Yes, but not so retroactive from the trauma of the event," argued Ericka. "His knowledge and memory seem to be of events primarily from the early 20th century. It was bits and pieces at first. Now it's become more intense since he was shown a book on Nikola Tesla. He insists that he has some connection to Tesla, and he filled a tablet with mathematical formulas."

"The book may have triggered the memory that he's a scientist," suggested Dr. Wolcott.

"That's what I thought at first," said Ericka. "I asked the physics teacher at the high school to take a look at his formulas. She said they were typical of scientific theories proposed in the late 1800s and early 1900s, mostly by Tesla. The kicker is that the patient has no knowledge of modern-day physics, Leanne."

Ericka gave a sigh of frustration. "He appears to be firmly rooted in 1903. It's where everything stops for him, and he can't seem to get beyond that point."

Dr. Wolcott twiddled a pen between her fingers, thoughtful for a moment.

"Tesla and his theories have been receiving a lot of attention lately especially among the younger scientists. That could trap your patient in that period of time," she conjectured.

"Or, maybe in addition to being a scientist, he's a history buff," the director continued, "and the memories he's accessing are actually knowledge he has gathered from studying that particular era."

"I considered all that, Leanne. If the latter is the case, he carried his immersion a bit too far."

"How so?"

"The patient was found wearing early 20th century clothes, and his handwriting actually resembles the penmanship of that era. Also, his vernacular is different," explained Ericka. "He doesn't understand the slang or lingo of today. It's as though whatever knowledge of the past he acquired has fused with his memory of present day."

"Hmm. That's a new wrinkle," admitted Dr. Wolcott. "Have you done all the screenings to rule out an organic cause of his amnesia?"

Ericka nodded. "EEG, CT, MRI, blood tests…all were normal. We had to have missed something."

The director smiled. "To quote Sherlock Homes, 'There is nothing more deceptive than an obvious fact.' Go home and get some rest, Ericka. Get a fresh perspective. Maybe you're over-thinking this."

Ericka stifled a yawn. "You're probably right." She stood up to leave. "Thanks for listening."

"Anytime. Let me know how the case progresses."

At the doorway, Ericka stopped. "Leanne, do you know a reporter, Kip Stevens?"

Dr. Wolcott nodded. "Yeah, sure. Everyone knows Kip."

"I'm not sure that's a ringing endorsement," remarked Ericka with a wry twist of her mouth.

The director laughed. "No, really. Kip is a good guy. Why do you ask?"

"He's the one who found my amnesia patient. He has built a rapport with him and has insinuated himself into the case."

Dr. Wolcott chuckled. "So that's why Stevens has been hanging around the hospital lately."

Ericka gave a huff of annoyance. "The man is like a dog with a bone. Short of banning him from the ward, I don't know what to do about him."

"Kip is a good investigative reporter," said Dr. Wolcott. "Until a year ago, he worked for the *Philadelphia Inquirer*. If he can track down some information on your patient, why not let him help?"

"He's interfering with the process of care, Leanne."

The administrator pursed her lips. "Hmm. Are you sure that's all it is?"

Ericka furrowed her brow. "What do you mean?"

"Oh, for heaven's sake, Ericka, don't tell me you haven't noticed what the other women in this town have," said Dr. Wolcott with a laugh. "Kip Stevens is the complete package—tall, dark, and handsome…great bod for a guy 40 something, good sense of humor. He'd be on my radar if I were 20 years younger."

Ericka snorted. "Really, Leanne? The man is arrogant."

"No…no, I think you're mistaking that for self-confidence," replied the director. She fixed a sharp eye on her staff member. "Not all good-looking guys are the scum of the Earth, you know."

"No, just 99% of them," retorted Ericka. "Narcissism is part of their genetic makeup. They have to cheat and lie to feed their egos."

"Is that your personal or professional observation?" questioned Dr. Wolcott with the lift of her brow.

Ericka was silent for a moment. "I wasted too many years in a relationship like that to know these guys can't change, Leanne."

"Maybe Stevens is the one percent that doesn't need changing."

Ericka gave a cynical laugh. "Fat chance. Who leaves the *Philadelphia Inquirer* for a small-town gazette?"

Dr. Wolcott shrugged. "I don't know the whole story, but apparently, he wrote a political expose that upset some important people and refused to take it back. I'd call that integrity."

"Is that your personal or professional observation?" mimicked Ericka.

Dr. Wolcott smiled. "Both—and I have years more experience. Give Kip a chance, Ericka. Let him help. He might surprise you."

CHAPTER TEN

WHAT HAPPENED TO RILEY HARRINGTON?

On his way out of Slaterville, Kip stopped by the nursing home to return the diary to Miss Maddie. When he arrived, he signed in at the desk. As he started down the hall to Maddie's suite, Jan the nurse hailed him.

"Mr. Stevens, Miss Maddie was admitted to the hospital last night. She was asking to see you this morning."

Kip looked at the woman in surprise. "She was fine when I left her yesterday. What happened?"

"With people Miss Maddie's age, when the time finally comes, it happens fast. I would suggest that you hurry, Mr. Stevens. I'll call ahead and let them know you are on your way."

Kip quickly drove across town. At the hospital, he was directed to the nurses' station on the third floor.

He had just stepped out of the elevator when a nurse walked up to him. "Are you Mr. Stevens?"

"I am," said Kip.

"Follow me. Miss Claymore is waiting for you, but she is fading fast."

When he walked into the room, Maddie's eyes fluttered open as though she sensed he was there. "Did you read the diary?" she asked, her voice barely above a whisper.

Kip nodded. "I did."

"And?"

"What happened to Elizabeth Slater?" he asked. "Julia's last passage was unclear to me."

"You'll find the answer. That's why you were chosen."

He let the comment slide. "Some of the pages of the diary are missing. They appear to have been torn out—"

Maddie grasped his hand. "Something has happened, Mr. Stevens. You must fix it."

Kip was surprised by the desperation in her tone. Mindful of her end-of-life state, he humored her.

"Fix what, Miss Claymore?"

"History, Mr. Stevens."

"How am I to do that?"

"Follow the signs," she whispered. Her eyes fluttered shut then, her energy drained.

The nurse asked him to wait in the waiting room. Twenty minutes later, the doctor came out and told him that Maddie had passed away. Kip felt strangely sad about it.

"Did you know her long?" the doctor asked.

"No, only for a few days," said Kip. "But she was that kind of person one doesn't forget," he added with a wry smile.

The doctor smiled as well. "Yes, Maddie was one of a kind. She was an institution in Slaterville. She rallied long enough to instruct me to give you this." He handed Kip a small leather bag. "She said you would know what to do with it when the time comes."

Kip opened the bag and saw that it contained silver coins. His brow knit in bewilderment. "It seems she had more faith in my talents of deduction than I do."

* * * * *

Ted Dittmore turned from editing an article on the computer when Kip strolled into his office. "Well, what did you find in Slaterville?" he asked with low expectations.

Kip tossed a form on his desk. "Enough for you to approve my expenses."

Dittmore scanned the voucher. "Five hundred dollars?!"

"It's tourist season, Chief."

Dittmore glared at Kip as he signed the form. "What did you find? It better be worth it."

Kip hesitated. "The matter is-uh-complicated. I need more time to chase some leads."

The editor snorted. "What else is new? Convince me."

Kip took out a photo and laid it on the desk. "Who do you see?"

"One of them looks like the guy you found on the side of the road," replied Dittmore. "So he *is* one of those re-enactors in the Slaterville celebration. What's so complicated about that? Case solved."

Kip smiled. "You're looking at a copy of a 1903 press photo from the Slaterville newspaper of Nikola Tesla and his assistant Riley Harrington."

Kip took out his cell phone and pulled up a picture of John. "This is our John Doe."

Dittmore's jaw dropped as he studied the two images. "What the hell—they look like the same man."

"Exactly. I thought Riley Harrington might be John's great grandfather or some direct descendent," said Kip. "But Harrington supposedly died in 1903 without any children."

"Why supposedly? Is there a question about it?"

"It depends on who you talk to," replied Kip.

"Jesus, Stevens, nothing is ever simple with you. Sit down and start at the beginning."

Kip pulled up a chair and sat down.

"In October of 1903, Nikola Tesla gave a series of lectures and demonstrations of his coil in Slaterville," explained Kip. "He brought along his assistant, Riley Harrington. In the course of events, Harrington met Elizabeth Slater, and it was love at first sight. Her father, who pretty much ran the town, wasn't happy about it, so the couple made plans to elope."

"Get to the end," ordered Dittmore.

"Her father found out about their plans, hired two drifters to rough up Harrington and force him to leave town," continued Kip. "But these guys got carried away and Harrington was shot. They claimed they hadn't killed him…that Harrington just disappeared."

"So, what's the mystery?" asked Dittmore. "The guy left town."

"According to the drifters, Harrington went poof," said Kip, gesturing with his hands.

"What do you mean he went poof?" the editor demanded to know.

"The drifters said there were lightning bolts, and he just disappeared into the jaws of hell."

Dittmore laughed. "They had to have been drinking to come up with a story like that."

"They were," admitted Kip. "But something strange did happen that night. By all accounts, the drifters were so terrified, they left behind the evidence that convicted them. Harrington's remains have never been found, and he never turned up after that point."

"Newspapers in those days were notorious for sensationalizing stories, and there was a high interest in the paranormal then," pointed out Dittmore. "What do transcripts of the trial say?"

"The judge held a closed hearing, and a fire destroyed all records from 1890 to 1908," replied Kip.

"Convenient but not uncommon," remarked the editor. "What about the newspapers?"

"There was only one newspaper," said Kip, "and it was short on detail. It seems the town fathers didn't welcome that kind of publicity at the time they were trying to woo outside investors."

"If Slater controlled the town, why would he bother to hire these drifters when he had a whole police force at his disposal?" Dittmore wondered aloud.

"I don't know. Maybe he needed patsies," said Kip. "I talked with an old man whose grandfather was on the police force at the time. He said his grandfather told him that it was later determined the two drifters hadn't killed Harrington, and they were released from prison in 1907, never to be heard from again."

Dittmore's brows knit in bewilderment. "So does that mean that someone else killed Harrington or that no one killed Harrington?"

Kip shrugged. "Your guess is as good as mine. Tesla went around the country giving lectures and demonstrations with electricity, amazing his audiences with what looked like bolts of lightning to them. As his assistant, Harrington would know the trick and be able to pull off a disappearing act with these two idiots none the wiser."

The editor ran a hand across his face as he considered the possibility. "That would take a lot of planning. Harrington would have to have advance knowledge of these characters' scheme."

"There was a solar storm occurring at the time with a vivid borealis," recalled Kip. "Scientists of the day understood the phenomenon, but people in rural areas didn't. The old man I spoke with said it had created some hysteria. Maybe Harrington just slipped away in the confusion."

"Maybe, but if Harrington was shot, he couldn't have gotten very far without help," said Dittmore. "And he would have needed a doctor. It's not likely that his whereabouts would have been a secret for long. Have you checked the censuses?"

Kip nodded. "Other than being listed in the 1900 census for Manhattan, there is no mention of Harrington after 1903. I even checked the 1910 federal census for counties in Pennsylvania, New Jersey and New York, where there were science labs, as well as the 1905 and 1915 state censuses for New York and New Jersey."

"What about the state census for Pennsylvania?" asked Dittmore.

"Pennsylvania didn't conduct state censuses," replied Kip.

Dittmore paused for a moment to think. "Maybe Harrington changed his name."

"I looked into that," said Kip. "When someone changes his name, he generally uses a variation of his real name and stays within his profession. I checked out the men Harrington's age in the censuses who listed their occupations as scientist, mathematician, teacher, professor. I got nothin'."

"Did you check marriage licenses?" quizzed Dittmore. "The guy could have been married when he came to Slaterville. Maybe Elizabeth Slater found out that he had a wife and hired these drifters herself to teach him a lesson."

"I found no evidence to suggest that," said Kip.

"Still, it doesn't mean there couldn't have been an illegitimate child," insisted the editor. "You said Elizabeth Slater's father hushed up everything right away. She could have been pregnant with Harrington's child and the baby put up for adoption."

Kip let out a heavy sigh. "I'm not sure of anything, Chief, but it was a small town, people still gossiped. There wasn't a hint of a whisper that Elizabeth Slater had a child out of wedlock. She didn't even have children with the man she later married."

Kip paused as another thought came to mind. "The town historian told me that Elizabeth Slater disappeared in 1907."

"She disappeared too!" exclaimed Dittmore.

"Some people thought that her husband might have done something to her," continued Kip. "There was a quiet investigation, but nothing was proven. Elizabeth's father had died the year before, and her father-in-law stepped in to fill the power vacuum. He put it around that she had left town and that was that."

"So? That's possible," said Dittmore. "What's the mystery?"

"Her bag was found at the train station, Chief. And Elizabeth's husband was in and out of a mental institution over the following years before finally killing himself—maybe because of a guilty conscience?"

"No one saw her get on the train?" quizzed Dittmore.

Kip shook his head.

The editor let out a low whistle. "Geez, Slaterville must have a pretty big closet to hide all those skeletons."

Kip rubbed his eyes, tired and scratchy from hours of reading. "If I had the missing pages from Julia Trowbridge's diary, it would probably answer a lot of questions."

"What diary and who is Julia Trowbridge?" asked Dittmore.

"She was Elizabeth Slater's confidante," replied Kip. "Julia's granddaughter gave me her grandmother's diary. But she died this morning before I could get any more information."

"Jesus, she died too?"

Kip gave him a wry look. "She was 96, Chief." He took out a pouch and emptied coins on the desk. "She also gave me these."

The editor picked up a couple of coins and examined them. "This is a 1902 Morgan silver dollar. And this is a 1900 Barber silver half dollar." He looked through the rest of them. "My God, you have several of these. I'm no expert, but these could be worth thousands of dollars."

Kip gathered up the coins. "I don't think she intended for me to sell them."

"Why would she give them to you?" asked Dittmore.

Kip shrugged. "I don't know. She said I would know what to do with them when the time came. She said a couple of other strange things—"

The editor put up a hand. "Stop, you're giving me a headache. Tell me when you have everything figured out."

"Does this mean that I'm still on the story, Chief?"

"For now," replied the editor grudgingly.

Kip grinned. "It gets its hooks into you, doesn't it? Four days ago, you threatened to fire me over it."

"Don't remind me. Now get the hell out of here before I change my mind. And don't forget the mayor's press conference tomorrow morning."

CHAPTER ELEVEN

A COMPLICATED SITUATION

Kip strode into the psych unit of the hospital and nearly collided with Dr. Porter. "Whoa, there. Where are you going in such a hurry? I was hoping we could grab some coffee and talk."

"Not today," she replied brusquely.

"How's John?" he asked.

"The same and anxious to see you. His room is three doors down on the right—number 316. Sorry, I have to go, Mr. Stevens."

She hurried off, and Kip walked down to the hospital room.

John rose from a chair and regarded Kip with high hope when Kip walked in. "Did you talk with Mr. Tesla?" he asked anxiously.

Kip was knocked off balance for a moment, still trying to get used to the fact that John's present was 1903. "Uh…not yet, but I did go to Slaterville," he replied.

He took out several photos from a manila folder and handed them to John. "I took these pictures around town. Does anything look familiar?"

John looked through a couple of the pictures. "These aren't of Slaterville," he declared. "The pictures look nothing like it. This isn't even the same town."

He tossed the photos on the bed and raked a hand through his brown hair in frustration. "Dr. Porter keeps trying to make me admit to things I know aren't true. Why do you try to fool me, too? I thought you were helping me."

"I am," said Kip. "And so is Dr. Porter in her own way, but the fact of the matter is there are things that don't make sense to any of us for different reasons. So, be patient. We have to work through this systematically together until we find the key that unlocks the truth."

John was silent for a moment. "You are right. Please accept my apology. I will try to be more patient."

His eye caught sight of one of the pictures scattered on the bed, and he picked it up. He quickly sifted through the rest of the pictures, finding more of the same, and laughed with giddy relief.

"This is Slaterville," he cried. "This is where I was."

Kip looked to see that John was focused on photos of the historic area—the town square, the historic homes, the theater. "Are you sure these are the only pictures of the town you recognize?" he asked, puzzled.

John nodded vigorously. "Yes. I know not the town of these other pictures…. I must go to Slaterville," he said with sudden urgency. "Can you take me there?"

Kip hesitated. "I don't know. Dr. Porter will have to okay it. What about your injuries?"

"My ribs and side are still a touch tender, but I am fit enough," John assured him.

"Okay, I'll speak with Dr. Porter and try to arrange a daytrip for next week, but don't get your hopes up."

"No, we must go tomorrow," insisted John.

Kip raised a brow. Tomorrow was Saturday—the start of his much-anticipated weekend date with pizza and football. "Can't this wait until Monday?" he asked.

John shook his head emphatically. "Time is of the essence. I cannot tell you how I know that. I just do. Please, we must go tomorrow."

Kip sighed. "I'll see what I can do."

Kip found Dr. Porter at the nurses' station filling out orders on an iPad.

"Dr. Porter, may I have a word with you?"

She handed the iPad to the nurse behind the desk. "Does it involve coffee, Mr. Stevens?"

Kip gave a faint smile. "This isn't social, Doctor. I need to discuss something with you regarding John."

"What about John?"

"He wants me to take him to Slaterville tomorrow," replied Kip. "We're almost the same size. I can bring him some clothes to wear."

Kip expected a stern lecture and a curt refusal. Instead, she took off her glasses and fixed him with a look he couldn't quite read.

"I'm going on break," she said to the nurse. "I'll be in the cafeteria. Mr. Stevens, you may buy me that coffee now."

As she started off, Kip stared after her in surprise. This was unexpected, and he had to hurry to catch up to her.

When they were settled at a table in the cafeteria, she immediately got down to business. "Now, Mr. Stevens, why does John want to go to Slaterville, and why does it have to be tomorrow?" she asked.

"John said he remembers being there and that time is of the essence," replied Kip.

Dr. Porter glanced askance at him. "He didn't say anything about this to me when I saw him this morning. Did you say or do something to trigger that memory, Mr. Stevens?"

"I just showed him some pictures I had taken the other day of Slaterville," replied Kip.

"And what was John's reaction?" she quizzed, stirring creamer into her coffee.

"He didn't recognize anything until he saw pictures of the historic area. It was then that he insisted that he had to go there," said Kip.

"Why did you go to Slaterville in the first place, Mr. Stevens?"

Kip smiled. "I think you missed your calling, Doctor. You should have been an interrogator."

She ignored the comment and repeated the question. "Why did you go to Slaterville?"

"Because John asked me to go," answered Kip.

Ericka looked at him in surprise. "John asked you to go? Why?"

"He saw the name of the town in the book I had brought him. He said that he had been there—with Tesla. And he asked me to go to Slaterville to see if anyone could identify him," explained Kip. "So, I went."

"I see," said Ericka. "And you didn't think that it might be important enough to tell me."

Kip detected an edge in her tone. "No—yes—I mean I wanted to check it out first," he said. "I'm a reporter. I follow leads. It's what I do."

"Mr. Stevens, I will remind you that John is my patient before he is your story!" she erupted in a low voice. "You do not get to make these kinds of decisions without consulting me first! You are not the arbiter of information in this case!"

"Doctor, I—"

"I'm not finished, Mr. Stevens. If you side-step my authority again, I'll have you barred from the floor. Do I make myself clear?"

Kip nodded, duly chastised. "Perfectly. Apologies, Doctor.... Don't you want to know what I found in Slaterville?"

Ericka set her coffee cup down with a huff of annoyance. The man really was irrepressible. "What did you find in Slaterville, Mr. Stevens?"

"The town is celebrating Founders' Day and people are dressed in period clothes," said Kip.

Ericka's gaze shot to him. "That would explain why John was wearing those clothes."

Kip allowed himself a smug smile. "Exactly. And guess what? Nikola Tesla had visited Slaterville in 1903 and did a demonstration on alternating current in the old theater. The Historical Society has set up re-enactments of the event there."

Ericka's eyes widened in amazement. "John was a re-enactor. It all fits. It would explain why he's confusing 1903 with present day. This is the piece of the puzzle I've been missing."

"You're welcome, Doctor."

"This doesn't excuse your actions, Mr. Stevens. What's John's real name?"

"I don't know," said Kip.

"What do you mean you don't know?"

"I showed John's picture around town, but no one knew who he was," said Kip. "Believe me, Dr. Porter, I am just as surprised and disappointed as you."

"Surprise and disappointment are not what I'm feeling right now, Mr. Stevens. After that build up, you cannot then tell me that someone didn't know him," she retorted sharply.

"Hold on." Kip pulled out his cell phone and opened it to the press photo. "Recognize anyone?"

Ericka looked at it, knitting her brows in confusion. "Then John was a re-enactor. Why didn't anyone know him?"

"Because this is the press photo of Tesla and his assistant Riley Harrington taken in 1903," said Kip, watching her reaction.

Surprise and disbelief flooded her features, soon displaced by anger again. "Is this a trick?! Did you not learn your lesson, Mr. Stevens?!"

"It's not a trick, Doctor. The photo is authentic."

She gave him a dubious look and studied the picture closer. "The resemblance is uncanny. Did you show this to John?"

Kip shook his head. "I didn't want to add to his confusion."

"Well, at least you got that right. This man must be John's great grandfather or some descendant."

"That's what I thought," said Kip. "But the guy appears to have died in 1903 under mysterious circumstances, and so far, I can find no evidence that he ever had a child or siblings."

Dr. Porter looked at the picture again. "That's not possible. You must have overlooked something."

"There's a lot of mystery surrounding Riley Harrington, Doctor, but I can assure you I left no stone unturned that I'm aware of."

Kip recounted to her what he had told his editor and explained about the diary, leaving out mention of Maddie Claymore's idiosyncratic musings.

Ericka shook her head, befuddled. "It doesn't make sense. If Riley Harrington hadn't died that day, I would think that he would have let Elizabeth know he was alive. And if he had any honor at all, he wouldn't have allowed those men to go to jail for a murder they hadn't committed."

"Well, they did beat him up, and one did shoot him," Kip reminded her. "They deserved to spend some time in jail…. You know what else is odd about all of this?"

Dr. Porter's brow rose. "There's more?"

"The stories of Harrington and Elizabeth parallel each other but four years apart," replied Kip.

"How so?"

"Well, Harrington ceased to exist in 1903 and was presumed dead, but no body was found. Elizabeth fell off the grid in 1907. There was some question that her husband might have had a hand in her disappearance, but, again, no body was found. Maybe knowing that her father would never let them be together, Elizabeth and Riley planned this elaborate scheme," surmised Kip.

Ericka dismissed the idea. "That's a pretty wild theory."

"No, think about it," insisted Kip. "Something happened in that grove that was crazy enough to distract and terrorize those drifters. What if, during all of this, Harrington managed to slip away and did get word to Elizabeth that he was alive? They had planned to run away before. Why not again? It would be easy to do if everyone thought they were both dead."

"Why would they wait four years?" questioned Ericka. "Why not run away before she married this other man?"

Kip sighed. "I don't know. Maybe her father was too much of a force to deal with. He was determined she should marry Thomas Marshall, the scion of Slater's elite equal. And from what I've heard, Slater always got his way. When her father died in 1906, Elizabeth and Riley saw their chance."

"They would not have been able to marry unless she divorced her husband or he died," Ericka pointed out.

"Maybe just being together was all that mattered to them," replied Kip. "John could be their descendant."

Ericka was still skeptical. "Riley and Elizabeth would have had to be in contact with each other the whole time to plan this. It's a stretch to think that they could carry on a secret relationship for that long without detection."

Kip couldn't debate that point. And from what he had read in Julia's diary, Elizabeth had been in despair over Harrington's disappearance. There was no indication there had been any contact between them, but what if that had been an act, too? Maybe this was what the missing pages in the diary were all about.

Aloud, he asked: "How else do you explain the strong resemblance between John and Tesla's assistant?"

"It's just one of those weird coincidences," replied Ericka. "It is said everyone has a twin."

Kip scoffed. "Over a century apart in time?"

"Okay, it's strange," she agreed, "but, unless you come up with something better, I'm sticking with coincidence. Not to change the subject, but why did you really choose to give John a book on Tesla?"

"I told you. I heard that he showed an interest in engineering and mathematical abilities. Tesla was a scientist." Kip shrugged. "It seemed a good fit."

"Why not a book about Einstein or some present-day physicist?" pressed Ericka.

Kip hesitated. "Promise not to laugh?"

"No, but tell me anyway."

Reluctantly, Kip told her about encountering the psychic at the police station. "I asked her about John. She said she felt that he had a connection with Tesla. I wanted to see if she was right."

Ericka regarded him with that look he couldn't read.

"The book did trigger a response when nothing else has," he pointed out.

"It's a false response, Mr. Stevens. John is mistaking historical facts for current memories, and I don't want to enable that misconception with any more references to a past time."

"I think you're overly concerned, Dr. Porter. John didn't read that much of the book."

"He read enough to think that he's Nikola Tesla's assistant," retorted Ericka.

"And it led to Slaterville," countered Kip.

"Where no one could identify him," she reminded him. "And regardless of the curious resemblance between the two men, Riley Harrington is old history and has nothing to do with John's case, so please let's not confuse the issue."

"What about John's request to go to Slaterville tomorrow?" asked Kip.

Dr. Porter was silent for a minute and, judging by the expression on her face, Kip would have bet against her saying "yes." She surprised him once again.

"I will allow the trip," she said, "but only if I accompany you and it is understood that I'm in charge, Mr. Stevens."

"Of course, Doctor."

"This is not a pleasure trip," she continued. "The purpose is to find a connection there that will snap John back to the present, not feed his fantasies of a life in an earlier day. You can do him great harm by indulging these delusions he's so reluctant to let go of."

"I understand," replied Kip. "By the way, John asked me if I had talked with Tesla…if Tesla had identified him."

Dr. Porter looked at Kip in alarm. "What did you say?"

"I said 'no.'" Kip leaned back in his seat and smiled. "You didn't tell John that Tesla is long dead, did you?" When she evaded his eye, he remarked, "It looks as though I'm not the only one enabling John's fantasies."

Dr. Porter glared at him. "The situation is complicated, Mr. Stevens. I warn you again, do not interfere in the process. Do we have an agreement?"

"We do," he replied. "Now, I have a condition of my own to put forward."

"I hardly think you're in a position to bargain, Mr. Stevens. What is your condition?"

"That if we're going to collaborate, you must call me Kip."

"We're not collaborating," she flatly retorted.

Kip cocked his head. "You still have no name for John, no identifier, just a lose connection to Slaterville—thanks to me. I have other leads, and with respect, Doctor, investigation is what I know and do well."

Ericka bit her lip. "Okay, you win—this time, Mr. Stevens."

"Kip," he corrected. "And…"

She looked at him. "You can continue to call me Dr. Porter."

"Turnabout is fair play, Doctor."

"I don't know you well enough, Mr. Stevens—"

"Kip."

"I don't know you well enough—Kip—nor do I care to."

"O-o-kay, we'll leave it there for now," he said. "A word of warning, Doctor, reporters are averse to rejection."

"So, I've gathered," she returned. She eyed him with curiosity. "I understand you're from Philadelphia and worked for the *Inquirer*. You're a big fish in a little pond here."

Kip smiled. "Have you been checking into me, Dr. Porter?"

Ericka huffed. "To the contrary, this is a small town. People like to talk. Why did you come here? I can't imagine what Fairfield has to offer you."

Kip shrugged. "I grew up in a small town. I like the mountains, and I needed to push the restart button…re-prioritize. With the university nearby, this area is becoming a vibrant R & D center. There's opportunity here for a fresh start. So, you see, we're not so very different, Dr. Porter."

"I beg your pardon?"

"Fed up with bureaucracy and politics, you left a prestigious job at Johns Hopkins to accept a position at the hospital here," said Kip.

Ericka blinked in surprise. "How do you—"

"It's a small town, Dr. Porter. People like to talk…. And as I've told you," he continued, his silver blue eyes locking on hers, "I'm good at getting facts when a subject interests me."

Ericka blinked not sure what to infer from that, and she abruptly rose from the table visibly disconcerted. "You may pick me up in front of the hospital tomorrow morning—nine o'clock. Please don't be late," she said and rushed off.

Kip smiled.

CHAPTER TWELVE

A FIELD TRIP

The next morning, John and Kip walked out of the hospital to Kip's car parked out front. John was in in awe. It looked nothing like the motorcars he was familiar with.

"What kind of motor does it have?" he asked.

"It's a hybrid," said Kip.

At the blank look on John's face, Kip explained. "It runs on electricity and gas." He lifted the hood. "Have a look."

John was amazed by the neat arrangement of boxes and hoses and became transfixed as Kip pointed out the motor and explained the general mechanics of the machine.

"Batteries in the back store the electricity," he said.

John reverently ran his hand over the top of the car. "What is this metal that forms the body of this carriage?"

Kip shrugged. "Steel and fiberglass, I guess."

"What is fiberglass?"

"It's a kind of plastic."

John looked at him blankly. "What is plastic?"

Kip gave a sigh of relief when Ericka drove up. "I'll explain later."

When she got out of the car, Kip did a double take. Her reddish-brown hair was pulled back in a ponytail, and she wore fashionable ankle boots and jeans and a fitted suede jacket that clearly outlined a shapely figure. He wasn't used to seeing her dressed in anything other than slacks and a doctor's coat, and it was a bit of a shock to his senses. He also noticed that she wore more makeup that accentuated her attractive features, giving her a more mature look.

"What's going on?" she asked, joining them.

"I was explaining about the car," said Kip, stealing glances at her.

Ericka frowned. "John shouldn't be out here with you. I haven't signed the release yet. I thought you agreed to respect the process."

"I have. But since *I* was on time and *you* were late," said Kip, giving her a pointed look, "Leanne signed the release so we could leave as soon as you arrived."

A blush stained her cheeks. "An accident," she replied.

Kip's mouth curved up in a smile of amusement. "What would you call that, Doctor—coincidence or fate?"

"I would call it Murphy's Law," she shot back.

John had walked over to her car and was examining it closely. "May I, Dr. Porter?"

Ericka looked at Kip in bewilderment.

"He wants to look under the hood of your car," said Kip. "Can you pop it?"

Still puzzled, she popped the hood.

Again, John marveled at the neat compartmentalization of the components. "I would like to take apart these boxes and see the parts…observe how they work," he said.

Ericka raised her brow at that, not amenable to having her car taken apart even to benefit a patient's recovery.

Kip smothered a grin and stepped in. "Perhaps another time, John. If we're going to Slaterville, we should get moving."

Just then an airplane flew low over head in its final descent to the nearby airport.

John looked up and took a step back, startled by the roar of the engines and the sight of such an object moving through the sky.

"What is that!" he exclaimed.

Kip and Ericka glanced at each other in surprise.

"It's an airplane," said Kip.

John put a hand to his forehead to shield his eyes from the sun and stared enthralled by the machine until it disappeared from sight.

He turned to Kip. "Man has been trying to devise a way to fly for thousands of years with the use of gliders. A machine as this I have never seen. How does it not fall from the sky?" he asked in awe.

Kip could see that Ericka was disturbed. "Ah…we'll discuss this another time, John. We should leave for Slaterville now."

John nodded, his imperative to reach the town taking priority over the scientific marvel he had just witnessed.

They got into Kip's car, and Kip started the engine. John sat in the backseat, further astounded by windows that went up and down with the push of a button and strange sounding music that came from no-where.

"I have never heard such music. From where does it come?" he asked, looking around him.

Ericka and Kip exchanged looks again.

"It's a radio," said Kip. "The music comes through speakers…from the dashboard," he explained, not the most mechanically minded.

"Mr. Tesla patented a wireless device that sends and receives radio waves for communication but not music," said John. "I must tell him about this."

"This was a bad idea," whispered Ericka to Kip. "It's too much too fast. He's over-stimulated."

"He doesn't seem traumatized by it," Kip whispered back. "Maybe it'll pull him into the 21st century."

Ericka shook her head. "I have to take him back to the hospital."

"You can't keep him hermetically sealed, Dr. Porter."

She bristled. "I'm not keeping him hermetically sealed. It's—"

"Yes, I know. It's a process. Look, John isn't going to encounter any more technology in Slaterville that he has already encountered here," pointed out Kip.

Ericka glanced at John as he worked the electric windows more fascinated than frightened by technology, as he had been when he first awoke in the hospital.

"Okay, we'll proceed as planned," she said with some hesitancy. "But I call the shots."

Shortly after 11 o'clock, Kip drove into Slaterville. When he got to Main Street, Dr. Porter turned her head to watch John's reaction. It was obvious that he was struggling with memories. Confusion, frustration, disconcertion scrolled across his face as he looked out the window.

"What are you thinking?" she asked him.

John shook his head, agitated. "This is not Slaterville. It looks like the other town that Kip showed me pictures of. Why did you bring me here? I told you time is of the essence."

"Easy, John. We'll come to it," said Kip.

Kip parked the car, and they got out. As they walked, John's reaction was much the same. This wasn't what he remembered. When they came to the historic district and the town square, John's face lit up and he ran over to the theater.

When Kip and Dr. Porter caught up with him, he turned to them. "I performed here—with Mr. Tesla. I must go inside."

The theater was closed, but the lobby was open to tourists.

John looked around and smiled. "Yes, this is how I remember it." He let out an audible sigh of relief. Here, at last, was tangible proof that he hadn't imagined everything.

He led Kip and Dr. Porter outside, eager to discover more proof that he wasn't crazy. He laughed aloud as two horse-drawn carriages passed by.

Watching John become more settled in these surroundings, Ericka was having misgivings again about the trip. She considered ending the excursion but determined it might have a more damaging effect if she forced John to leave now. For the first time since he had become her patient, he seemed happy and connected.

When they came to the Slater Home, he stopped and stared at it. "Elizabeth," he murmured. Suddenly, he bolted up the steps and ran into the house shouting. "Elizabeth! Elizabeth, where are you!"

Startled, Kip and Ericka rushed after him.

John ran from room to room, shouting Elizabeth's name, pushing aside the barriers, startling the tour guide and frightening tourists. Caught up in another reality, he seemed not to even notice them. Kip finally took him in tow as Mrs. Rappaport came hurrying from the back of the house at the commotion.

She looked at Kip, surprised to see him. "Mr. Stevens, what is happening here?"

"I'm sorry, Mrs. Rappaport, there has been a mistake." He gave her an apologetic smile as he explained that John had been away for a long time and mistook the house for another.

As Kip and Ericka quickly hustled him outside, John protested. "I'm not mistaken."

"She isn't here," said Kip.

"Where is she?" cried John.

"Who? Will someone explain to me what is going on?" demanded Ericka, unnerved.

Kip took her aside. "This was Elizabeth Slater's house in 1903. John is looking for her."

Ericka looked at him dumbfounded. "How does John know about Elizabeth Slater?"

"I don't know. I didn't mention her to him," said Kip.

"This is enough for one day. We're returning to Fairfield now," Ericka announced aloud, her stance firm.

John balked. "No, I cannot leave!"

"We'll talk about this at the hospital—"

"No! I have to find Elizabeth, Dr. Porter."

Kip stepped in. "If it is as urgent for you to find Elizabeth as you feel it is, we're wasting time this way. We need to return to the hospital and come back with a plan."

After a few tense moments, John acquiesced.

The mood was subdued, conversation forced as Kip drove out of town. The main road was blocked for the start of a parade, so he had to take the old route leading out of Slaterville.

He had driven only a few miles when John suddenly became excited. "Kip, stop! Turn down that road."

Kip brought the car to a halt. It wasn't much of a road that John indicated but more a rutted path that hadn't been used in a long time. He looked at Ericka for a decision. She hesitated, then nodded, and Kip slowly turned onto the dirt road.

"Are you sure about this, John?" he asked as they bounced along.

"Keep going, Kip. It is here."

Half a mile further, they came to an overgrown orchard.

"This is it," said John.

Kip stopped the car, and John jumped out and ran over to an area of tall grass and blighted crabapple trees. Ericka and Kip got out of the car and looked around. The air was unnaturally still, not a whisper of a sound.

Exchanging looks of ill ease, they started after John. Suddenly, Kip stopped. The hair on the back of his neck stood up and his body tingled. The ground beneath his feet hummed.

"Do you feel that?" he asked Ericka.

She looked at him wide-eyed. "I thought it was just me."

"Look at your watch," said Kip.

She looked at her digital wristwatch and gasped. "It says 9 p.m."

Kip took out his cell phone. It was speedily scrolling through programs. "My phone is going crazy."

"Mine too," said Ericka. "What is this place?"

"It must be the grove Herbert Whitley told me about," replied Kip. "He said people are afraid to come here, that animals have disappeared."

Ericka scanned the field, unnerved again. "We should get out of here."

Kip nodded. "You won't get an argument from me."

John yelled then and motioned for them to come. "Over here!"

Eager to collect their charge and leave, Ericka and Kip hurried over to him.

"This is where I was shot," said John.

CHAPTER THIRTEEN

MORE QUESTIONS THAN ANSWERS

Monday morning, Kip walked briskly into police headquarters. He took the stairs two at a time to the second-floor detectives' enclave.

"Hey, Gillespie," he called out striding across the room.

The detective quickly put away the hand mirror he was using to adjust his toupee. "Geez, Stevens, do you have radar or something?" he groused irritably. "The ballistics report just came back from Harrisburg. Give me a minute."

"That's not why I'm here," said Kip. "I have some information for you. I drove John and his psychiatrist to Slaterville Saturday. Coming back, John directed us to an abandoned grove."

"Yeah, so," replied the detective, rifling through a drawer. "You can never find a pen when you need one," he grumbled. "Procurement seems to think you don't need pens and pencils with computers."

"Hank! John said he was shot there…in the grove."

Gillespie stopped searching and looked up at Kip. "No shit. Did you find evidence of it?"

"No, but John is certain that it's the place," said Kip.

"Huh. I'll contact Slaterville police and run over there for a look see. Does he remember anything else?"

Kip hesitated. "Nothing relevant."

The detective leaned back in his chair, thoughtful. "You know, Stevens, I hear the town is having one of those Founders' Day celebrations.... And the guy was wearing those old-fashioned clothes when you found him. If he was shot in the grove, he must have a connection to Slaterville."

"Gee, do you think?" responded Kip dryly. "Why do you think we went to Slaterville?"

Gillespie glared at him. "Did anyone recognize him?"

"No. He seemed familiar with the historic district, but not with the rest of Slaterville," said Kip. "He's probably a history buff from out of town who came to take part in the celebration and crossed paths with the wrong person."

Gillespie picked up the ballistics report and scanned it. "Then it was with another history nut that he crossed paths. This says the bullet taken out of your John Doe is from a Colt M1900 .38 handgun." He looked up at Kip. "The gun was manufactured in 1900."

Kip's jaw dropped. "Are you sure?"

The detective handed him the report. "See for yourself. Now, all I have to do is find a guy in the area that collects antique guns."

Kip quickly left the police station and arranged to meet Ericka at the Green Bean coffee house in half an hour. She was already there with her hands wrapped around a large cup of coffee when he arrived.

"Sorry, I had to order," she said as Kip sat down in the seat across from her. "I haven't slept well since the trip to Slaterville. The feeling I got in that old grove—my watch...the cell phone—I haven't been able to get any of it out of my mind."

The old grove hadn't left Kip's thoughts either. "It was probably some kind of electromagnetic pulses. Solar storms can alter Earth's magnetic field and cause currents to surge."

"But the storm is over," noted Ericka.

"There are probably still some geomagnetic aftershocks."

Ericka looked at him with a mixture of surprise and relief. "When did you become a scientist?"

"I wrote an article on the subject once. Has John remembered anything more?"

Ericka shook her head. "But his concern for Elizabeth has increased his level of agitation."

"Detective Gillespie is going to contact Slaterville police and make a search of the grove," said Kip.

"John has exhibited false memories before," she warned. "It could be a wild goose chase."

"Maybe, maybe not." Kip paused. "I have some news you may not want to hear."

Ericka groaned and fortified herself with more coffee. "What is it?"

"Gillespie showed me the ballistics report. John was shot with a gun manufactured in the year 1900," relayed Kip.

Ericka looked at him in disbelief. "You've got to be kidding."

Kip shook his head. "Gillespie is searching for someone in the area with an antique gun collection."

She threw up her hands in exasperation. "Will this box never square?"

"Maybe we're making too much of this," said Kip. "It could be just the misreading of a careless accident or an overheated argument. These history enthusiasts can sometimes get carried away. Whoever shot John probably thought he had killed him, panicked and dumped him along the side of the road."

"You're forgetting about the beating. I don't think that was by accident," replied Ericka with a wry smile. "And John was dumped on the road between Addison and Fairfield, not Slaterville and Fairfield. Nice try though."

"Well, it is a plausible explanation for the vintage clothes and the antique gun," maintained Kip.

"Except that no one in Slaterville knows John—and now he has this new obsession with Elizabeth Slater," Ericka reminded him. "Everything should fit but doesn't."

She sighed. "John is not following the psychological assessments of dissociative amnesia. The more I try to coax him into the present, the more he connects to the past." She eyed Kip closely "You're certain you didn't mention Elizabeth Slater to him?"

Kip gave her the three-finger promise. "Scouts honor. Look, re-enactors travel the country to events. That's why no one knows John. He's from out of town. He probably saw pictures of Elizabeth while touring the house like I did."

Ericka shook her head in frustration. "It's always one step forward and two steps back." She looked at her watch. "I have to get back to the hospital."

She stood up, and Kip rose to hold her coat for her.

"How about dinner tonight?" he asked.

Ericka gave him that appraising look he could never quite read.

"A working dinner, not a date," he clarified.

"Let's keep it to coffee," she replied. "But you may call me Ericka."

Kip smiled to himself. The wall was cracking.

He walked her back to the hospital and went on to the newspaper office. The newsroom was empty, and he sat down at his desk to think while he still had some peace and quiet. With a deadline approaching, the room would be a beehive of activity soon.

He opened a drawer and took out a rubber ball, tossing it between his hands as he considered where to go from here in his quest to uncover John's identity.

He was so deep in thought he jumped when his cell phone rang. He was surprised to see that the caller was Dr. Porter and quickly answered it.

"Ericka, did you change your mind about dinner tonight?" he asked, throwing the ball in the air and catching it.

"No. I'm calling to tell you that John remembered his name," she replied.

"No kidding. You sound upset. Isn't that a good thing?" questioned Kip, tossing the ball in the air again.

"He says he's Riley Harrington, Kip."

Kip went still, and the ball bounced on the floor.

"Are you there?" asked Ericka. "Did you hear what I said?"

"Yeah…yeah, I heard," Kip replied. "I'm just trying to wrap my head around it."

"Did you mention that name to John at any time?" she demanded to know.

"No, only to you," Kip assured her. "I don't know where he would have seen or heard the name Riley Harrington. Did you ask him?"

"He said it just came to him."

"Was there any mention of the name in the book I gave him on Tesla?" asked Kip.

"No. It was the first thing I checked," said Ericka.

"Then John must have heard it when we were in Slaterville," surmised Kip.

"How? We were with him the whole time."

Kip thought for a minute. "He could have seen the picture of Riley Harrington in the Slater house before his amnesia—"

"And remembered the resemblance," added Ericka. "He's confusing his life with Riley Harrington's. It makes sense. But how would John know about Riley and Elizabeth's romance? Could he have seen the diary?"

"I can't imagine how," said Kip. "You know I could write one heck of a story. Readers love a mystery like this. I have a contact at AP who could put the story out on the wire. It'll get national attention…. Hell, it could go viral on the internet—"

"You can't do that!" exclaimed Ericka.

Kip was taken aback. "Why not? A story like this could bring out someone who knows the truth."

"It will bring out fringe elements with crazy theories, Kip. You know as well as I do that stories of this nature excite the imagination.

You'll place John in the middle of a media frenzy that will do more harm than good."

"Okay, okay. You win," said Kip.

Ericka sighed. "Back to square one. Where do we go from here?"

Kip could hear the stress in her voice. "We'll figure it out."

When Ericka hung up, she wasn't feeling reassured. The clothes, the bullet, the photo, John's memories of another era and his strange behavior at the Slater House and the grove—she nearly laughed aloud. She knew what her sister would say about this—John was the reincarnation of Riley Harrington.

She and Patty had debated the concept enough times, both remaining steadfast in their opposing beliefs. She, Ericka, was a scientist for God's sake. How could she believe in such a thing? And yet, how could one argue the fact that John had the memories of another man's life? There had to be another explanation…a hoax perhaps. But for what reason? And there would have to be another person or persons involved. John didn't beat and shoot himself.

For Kip's part, Ericka had thrown him a curve ball he never expected, and he sat staring at the wall, the cell phone still clutched in his hand. Like her, his mind sifted through all the possibilities. There were a lot of pieces to the puzzle that refused to fit—unless there was another puzzle they weren't seeing.

A thought suddenly came to Kip, and he called Herbert Whitley in Slaterville with a question. The elderly man thought for a moment and came back with an answer that set Kip back on his heels.

CHAPTER FOURTEEN

MORE PIECES BUT TO WHICH PUZZLE?

Kip found Ericka sitting in a booth at the back of the coffee house, staring into space, her coffee barely touched.

"The hospital said I would find you here," he said, sliding into the seat across from her.

Ericka looked at him, the dark smudges beneath her eyes a telltale sign that she still wasn't sleeping well.

"I'm good at what I do," she said, her voice wavering with uncertainty. "I'm highly trained, and I have no idea what to think of John or do with him."

She took a sip of coffee.

"My mother warned me that it was dangerous to get into other people's heads when we don't know our own minds."

"You're being too hard on yourself," said Kip. "John's isn't an easy case."

Ericka gave a half-hearted laugh. "Nowadays, if people heard this story, they would believe he was the reincarnation of Riley Harrington, or that little gray men had abducted Harrington and dropped him along the side of the road over a hundred years into the future for you to find. I have a sister who believes in that kind of stuff."

Ericka took another sip of coffee. "I think I would much rather believe that John is playing us."

"I don't think he manufactured that 1903 photo," said Kip.

"Maybe it was photo-shopped."

Kip shook his head. "It was the same photo that appeared in the newspaper."

"What *are* you saying then?" she asked irritably. "You can't possibly believe John is Riley Harrington."

When Kip didn't answer, she looked at him incredulous. "Oh, no, don't tell me you believe that."

"Listen, I called a man whose grandfather was on the police force when the Harrington business went down," said Kip. "He told me that the two drifters tore into town with their story sometime after 8 p.m."

"So, what does that prove?" challenged Ericka.

"Daylight Savings Time went into effect in March of 1918, which means that Harrington would have been shot sometime around 9 o'clock Daylight Savings Time—8 p.m. 1903 time," explained Kip. "Do you remember the time our watches stopped in the grove?"

Ericka gave a short laugh. "Oh, come on. That's really a stretch even for you."

Kip shrugged. "Can you explain why John's wounds are the same as Harrington's? How else would John know those details?"

Ericka massaged her eyes. "I don't know. Sociopaths are good at manipulation and will go to great lengths to achieve their ends, even to the point of injuring themselves."

"C'mon, Ericka, you can't think John is a sociopath."

"He seems to want to remember," she admitted. "He exhibits the normal frustration and anger at not being able to recall events, but we'll see. He has agreed to undergo hypnosis next week."

Kip looked at her in surprise. "Hypnosis? I wouldn't have thought that to be a tool in your arsenal."

"It isn't. But the hypnotist is a professor from the Behavioral Science department of the college, and I've tried everything else."

"Mind if I sit in?" asked Kip.

"You'll have to get John's consent." Ericka shook her head in frustration. "The more I search for practical answers, the more I'm met with the improbable. Leanne thinks I'm over-thinking the case."

"It's hard to argue facts as strange as these," said Kip. "Let's see what comes from the hypnosis session."

* * * * *

John lay on his bed in a hypnotic trance. A heavy-set man with a gray beard and full head of hair that could use the talents of a good barber, sat on a chair next to him.

Ericka and Kip sat in the background as the professor led John into a hypnotic state.

"I want you to go back to the last place you remember being just before waking up in the hospital," he said.

"I'm in a grove," answered John.

"What is your name?" asked the professor.

"Riley Harrington."

"What's the date?"

"1903." John grimaced. "Two men are beating me."

"Why are they beating you?"

"I don't know…. I was supposed to meet Elizabeth."

Kip scribbled a question on a piece of paper and handed it to the professor.

The professor looked at it. "Who is Julia Trowbridge?"

"Elizabeth's closest friend," replied John.

Ericka looked at Kip curiously as he handed the hypnotist two more questions.

"What does she think of your relationship with Elizabeth?" the hypnotist asked.

"I don't think she approves, but she helps us," said John.

The hypnotist glanced down at Kip's other question. "Did something strange happen in the grove?"

John moved his head from side to side becoming agitated again. "Lightning…screaming…gunshots." John moaned. "Pain in my side…pulled backwards…everything is black."

"What's the next thing you remember?" questioned the hypnotist.

"In a hospital…machines I've never seen." John's face screwed up in confusion. "Everything looks different…. It's a different time."

"What time is it?" asked the professor.

"The 21st century, I am told."

"What's your name?"

"Riley Harrington."

The professor paused, startled for a moment. "Your name is Riley Harrington—in the 21st century?"

"Yes."

"Why are you in the hospital at this time?"

"I was beaten…and shot."

"By whom?"

"Two men."

Again, the professor paused, his brows knit in bewilderment.

"In the 21st century?"

"No, in 1903."

"That's enough," said Ericka. "Bring him out of it, Professor Nolan."

When the professor brought him out of the trance, John was confused and upset. "I thought this was supposed to make everything clear, Dr. Porter. I don't understand anything. Where is Elizabeth?"

Ericka quickly moved to calm him. "The brain is very complicated. Amnesia is tricky. A treatment that may work for one person may not work for another. We just have to find the right one for you. We'll figure it out, John."

"My name is Riley."

Dr. Porter hesitated. "Uh, we'll leave you to rest now." She signaled for Kip and the professor to follow her out of the room.

When they were in the hall, the professor shook his head. "I have to tell you, Dr. Porter, I have never seen anything like this before. It sounds like a case of past life memories, but usually memories this strong are seen only in children."

He thought for a moment. "This could be a case of bilocation where the body occupies one place and the mind another. It's been a belief held for centuries and has gained widespread recognition in the 21st century," he said, noting the skepticism on Ericka's face. "There are numerous studies, Dr. Porter."

"Yes, I'm aware," replied Ericka.

The professor furrowed his brow, nonplussed. "I've never heard of a case of bilocation in different time periods though, or where the experience has lasted this long." His eyes lit up with excitement. "This could be a new form of time travel. Dr. Porter, I would like to explore this more with your patient."

Ericka inwardly cringed. "Perhaps later. He's still recovering from his injuries you understand." She hustled him to an open elevator. "Thank you for coming, Dr. Nolan."

"I'll call," he said as the doors closed on him.

Ericka groaned and turned to Kip. "I could use a drink. Care to join me?"

Kip nodded. "Yeah, I do."

They walked the two blocks to the Fairfield Brewery. Kip guided her to a booth in the corner, stopping at the bar along the way to order two Scotch and sodas.

"I had hoped the session with the hypnotist would answer a few questions, not create more," she said with a heavy sigh as she slipped off her coat. "Now John is more confused than ever, and I'm out of options."

"I might have one more," said Kip.

She looked at him hopefully. "What?'

"You're not going to like it."

"If it has anything to do with bilocation, forget it."

"It doesn't, but you aren't going like it much better," warned Kip.

The waitress arrived with their drinks, and Ericka took a bracing sip of her Scotch.

"What is it?"

"Why don't you give the psychic I told you about a try?"

Ericka met his suggestion with the same skepticism that she had met the professor's idea of bilocation, and Kip considered that maybe he should have waited until she had taken a few more sips of her drink before making the suggestion.

"I know, I know. I was skeptical at first, too," he said. "But you have to admit the woman was spot on about Slaterville and John's connection to Tesla."

"Look, Kip, I took a leap with hypnotism. And you saw how well that worked out. A psychic doesn't come near to being on my list of acceptable treatments. I think John is so desperate to find his identity, he seized on the first person he came across—Riley Harrington."

"Ericka, I told you. I didn't show him the photo of Tesla's assistant, and I never mentioned Harrington's name to him. John couldn't have known about him or Elizabeth."

"Unless this whole thing is an elaborate hoax," interjected Ericka.

"Back to that now…for what reason?" questioned Kip.

"I don't know—publicity, maybe. You said John could be an actor. He saw this as a way to boost his career."

"That's pretty thin."

"Why? You came up with information on Harrington easily enough. So could have John. He was in town as a re-enactor, and like you said, could have seen the newspaper photo of Harrington, noticed the strong resemblance, and concocted this whole story right down to the detail of the injuries."

"So, John arranged to have someone beat and shoot him," remarked Kip dryly. "He would have died along the side of the road had I not come along when I did, Ericka."

"As I said, sociopaths will risk much to achieve their goals," she persisted. "Maybe the psychic was in on this. She's the one who led you to Slaterville and Tesla, and John took it from there once you took the bait."

Kip gave her a droll smile. "For the record, Ericka, I'm not that easily led. I talked with the librarian in Slaterville. No one has ever requested the microfiche of the 1903 newspapers but me.

"And under your scenario," he continued, "we would have to assume that the town historian is part of the scheme as well. I can't say that I would have noticed Riley in the photo if she hadn't pointed him out to me. That's a big cast of characters and the measures pretty extreme for just a publicity stunt."

"Then one would have to say that John is Riley Harrington," said Ericka. "I'm sorry. I can't accept that."

Kip sighed. "We're going in circles. Look, all those things I told you about Riley and Elizabeth's romance, and the questions I gave the hypnotist to ask John…that information was not known to anyone but Riley, Elizabeth, Julia Trowbridge, Maddie Claymore, and me. And except for me, they're all deceased."

"How do you know that this Claymore woman didn't share her grandmother's diary with other people?" quizzed Ericka.

"I don't," admitted Kip, "but I'm pretty certain that she didn't, and I don't think that she and John colluded to perpetrate a hoax either. No one working at the nursing home where she lived recognized John as being a visitor."

"You're right. We're going in circles," she murmured.

Both fell silent, centering their attention on their drinks for the moment.

"Ericka, do you believe that things happen for a reason…that a higher arching purpose can bring random events together?" Kip asked at length.

She replied with a flat out "No."

"Why not?" he challenged. "If I remember my psychology correctly, Freud believed in determinism."

"Einstein didn't," retorted Ericka.

"Then you would have to believe that there's never a purpose to anything," said Kip.

Ericka shook her head. "Not necessarily. Purpose is shaped by chance events, which are often misconstrued to be fate."

"Before John, I might have agreed with you," said Kip. "Now, I'm not so sure."

Ericka was adamant. "There's a rational answer for all of this…. There *has* to be."

Kip took a swig of his drink. "Why?"

"Because without rationality, there's chaos."

"No matter if the calculation is right or wrong?" he asked.

She regarded him through narrowed eyes. "What are you getting at?"

"There was a time when people thought it rational to believe the sun revolved around the Earth…that the Earth was flat…that—"

"Okay, I get your point, Kip. What does this have to do with John?"

"I wonder if there's something we're not grasping about this case, Ericka, because it isn't rational to us at this point in time."

CHAPTER FIFTEEN

THE ASSIGNMENT

"Hey, Stevens, the chief wants you to take this story," said the assistant editor.

"What is it?" asked Kip preoccupied with a task.

"There's a daylong science festival tomorrow at the university. They're bussing in high school students to get them more interested in pursuing careers in science. Dittmore wants you to run over to the university to cover it."

Kip looked up at the assistant editor. "What's wrong with Beasley? The nerd land stuff is his beat. I have other things to do."

"Beasley is out with the flu."

"Geez, half the staff is out with the flu. I'm already doing double duty, Adams. Can't Dittmore find someone else to send? What about Linda?"

"She's covering the mayor's political fundraiser, and no, you can't switch assignments with her. Dittmore doesn't want you near the place. The mayor wasn't too happy with the last piece you did on him."

Kip snorted. "I thought journalism was supposed to be about the truth."

"It's about diplomacy and timing as well, Stevens…something I thought you would have learned after the ruckus you caused in Philadelphia."

The assistant editor dropped the assignment sheet on Kip's desk. "You have half a page including photo. Buck up, Stevens. You might learn something about science."

* * * * *

Kip sat slouched in a seat at the back of the university lecture hall, prepared to be bored again. He had snoozed through biology and chemistry and needed more copy than student interviews could afford. Quantum physics was the only lecture left. It suddenly came to him that he hadn't planned this out very well. He had barely made it out of physics class.

Guest lecturer Dr. Robert D. Garson, a noted physicist according to the biography Kip had read, stepped up to the podium. He was a slight unassuming man of middle years with gray hair, a close-cropped beard, and wire-rim glasses—the glasses of choice for professors and science geeks, thought Kip. And why did scientists always have beards? Instead of the patched tweed jacket of academicians though, Dr. Garson was casually dressed in a plaid button-down Oxford shirt and khaki pants.

As with his dress, his manner was casual as he welcomed the students and invited them to participate in the lecture with questions and comments. He began with a few science jokes that even Kip found amusing, setting a comfortable tone in the hall.

"Physics is boring," stated Garson to the surprise of his audience. "That's right. You heard me correctly. And scientists can be pretty stuffy and closed-minded. They have a frame of comfort in which they like to work. They don't like to see established rules of science upended."

"However, quantum mechanics," he said with a twinkle in his eye, "is science of another order. It is the stuff of fiction that often becomes reality in the future like space exploration—and interstellar travel."

Hands immediately shot up.

"Interstellar travel is impossible, except by robot probes," stated one boy categorically. "You would have to travel faster than the speed of light and that's not possible—unless you're Captain Kirk and the Enterprise," he added to the laughter of the students. "Einstein said there's nothing faster than the speed of light."

The professor was undaunted. "That's true, according to the laws of gravity that we understand. But what about a shortcut through space-time…a tunnel through the universe that connects different places and different times?" challenged Garson.

"If you're talking about black holes, they aren't stable enough. They end in singularity," chimed in another boy.

Garson smiled. "Correct, but *wormholes* don't end in singularity."

"Wormholes don't exist. They're a myth," interjected a girl.

"How do you know that?" asked Garson.

"Has anyone ever seen a wormhole?" questioned another student.

"No," admitted the professor.

"Then how do you know they exist?"

Garson scribbled a mathematical formula on the chalkboard. "That is how I know," he said pointing to the equation. "This tells me that there is a high probability that wormholes exist."

At looks of confusion on the students' faces, Dr. Garson chuckled. "Welcome to the world of quantum mechanics. It makes the intangible world visible and the unthinkable thinkable. It's the mystery of Nature unveiled by mathematics.

"In quantum physics, rationality does not always apply," continued the professor. "It's a bit like teenagers. It likes to break the rules of established order. It is the world inside an atom that often times makes theoretically possible that which science cannot. In other words, quantum mechanics forces one to think outside the box."

Hands shot up again.

"You said wormholes connect space and time. Are you saying someone can really travel into the future?" asked another boy, doubtful.

"If space and time are connected as the consensus holds, then yes, it is theoretically possible," said Garson.

"What do you mean by theoretically possible? Either we can do it, or we can't, Dr. Garson."

"There's nothing in the laws of physics that prohibits us from travelling into the future—or back into the past," maintained Garson. "We just haven't figured out how to put it into practice yet."

"Einstein said that we can only move forward in time," argued a female student.

The physicist smiled, unfazed. "In 1949, Kurt Gödel discovered a solution to Einstein's field general relativity equations that allowed for the possibility of CTCs—closed time-like curves."

"What are they?" asked several students in unison.

"Space-time is not linear as many scientists first thought," explained Garson. "It loops back upon itself, thus allowing for time travel backwards through traversable wormholes, which are wormholes that can be traveled in both directions of time. Traversable wormholes were first proposed in 1988."

He drew a picture on the blackboard of a "u" shaped tube with a mouth at both ends.

"When the mouths of the wormhole are located near each other in space but separated in time, the wormhole can act as a time tunnel. In fact, it is generally held that naturally occurring wormholes most likely *are* time tunnels."

"I can go back to the age of dinosaurs?" asked an incredulous student.

"Only if one of the mouths of the wormhole is connected to that time period," replied Garson. "General Relativity doesn't allow one to travel back further than the point of creation of the time tunnel."

Garson pointed to another student with her hand raised. "Yes, young lady?"

"Don't you need some kind of time machine, Professor?"

"According to Gödel, the universe as a whole *is* the time machine. There's no need to build one," the professor replied.

This evoked murmurs of excitement among the students.

"But what about the law that says you can't go back in time because you might change something that could affect the future?" asked another female student.

"Yeah, and you might not exist," interjected a boy.

"Ah…you are talking about the grandmother paradox," said Garson. "You accidentally kill your grandmother and are never born."

"Yeah, that's it."

Garson smiled. "Novikov's Self Consistency Principle takes care of that problem. It does not permit the time traveler to change the past, however it does allow him to affect events as long as it doesn't cause inconsistencies in the original history."

There was quiet in the auditorium as the students worked to absorb everything.

"This all sounds like science fiction fantasy," scoffed another student. "Are you pulling our leg, Professor?"

Garson laughed. "I assure you, young man, I am not. Much of science has its roots in fantasy and much truth can be found in fiction."

"You said that wormholes occur naturally. How?" asked a girl.

"Many physicists are convinced that densities of negative energy exist in nature," explained Garson. "Using the quantum foam hypothesis that tiny wormholes exist in space, physicists have hypothesized that tiny wormholes, held open by negative-mass cosmic strings, were created at the time of the Big Bang and inflated to macroscopic size by cosmic inflation. And the universe is ever expanding."

"Then why haven't any wormholes been found?" another student demanded to know.

"The universe is a big place. Who's to say they haven't?" quizzed Garson. "Some scientists believe that many have been mistaken for black holes. And in 2008, NASA discovered hidden portals where Earth's magnetic field connects with the magnetic field of the sun.

"NASA is planning a mission to send four spacecrafts to study them," continued Garson. "But we do know the portals open and close several times every day and that some are so large and sustained they provide a direct path from our planet to the atmosphere of the sun. Who knows what other pathways they may offer to other dimensions or planets?"

Kip looked around the hall. The kids were listening with rapt attention, some with open-mouth astonishment.

"What would indicate the existence of a wormhole?" asked one of the girls.

"The way light is affected by the gravity of the wormhole and the electromagnetic field energy where there is a net flux of lines of force," replied Garson.

Kip's attention swiveled back to the professor, the Slaterville grove leaping to mind. He wanted to hear more on the topic, but Garson looked at the clock on the lectern and announced that time was up.

"I hope this lecture will encourage many of you to pursue a career in quantum physics," he said in closing. "Remember, every day science makes new discoveries that challenge our perception of reality and the very nature of our existence. Never be afraid to imagine the unimaginable.

"Discovery begins with dialogue," he continued. "As Ralph Waldo Emerson said: 'Do not go where the path may lead, go instead where there is no path and leave a trail.'"

The students gave the physicist a rousing ovation.

As they filed out of the lecture hall, Kip made his way to the front. "Dr. Garson, interesting lecture."

Garson looked up from the gathering of his papers. "Thank you. You don't look like a student. Are you a scientist?"

"No. I'm Kip Stevens, a reporter from the *Fairfield Gazette*. Were you just trying to inspire interest in science among the students or do you really believe time travel is possible?"

"I don't think that it is. I know that it is," responded Garson.

Kip was surprised by the physicist's conviction. "All you have is theory, Professor. That's a lot to take on faith, isn't it?"

Dr. Garson smiled. "One takes religion on faith, Mr. Stevens. The world of quantum physics is real. Not even God violates its laws. If a hypothesis isn't true, it won't be able to be solved mathematically. It's as simple as that. Mathematics never lies. But if you were to ask me if time travel is doable, I would have to say 'no'—at least not at this point in time."

"You seem to have omitted that fact in your lecture, Doctor."

"I never destroy a dream, Mr. Stevens. Therein lies the genesis of creativity and the genius of invention."

"May I quote you on that?"

"Of course."

"You said that a field of energy could indicate the presence of a wormhole. Would this field of energy be easily detectable?" asked Kip.

"It would depend on the size of the wormhole," replied the physicist. "If it was large enough, the energy field could emit strong electrical impulses."

"Enough to make a digital watch or cell phone go haywire?" pressed Kip.

Dr. Garson nodded. "Of course."

Kip took out his cell phone and pulled up one of several mathematical equations John had scribbled. "What can you tell me about this?"

Garson studied the equation for a minute. "This is an old equation for AC electric current...looks like early Tesla. Nikola Tesla was a brilliant physicist in the late 19th century and first half of the 20th century. Many of our inventions today are thanks to him."

"Yes, I know. I'm well acquainted with Nikola Tesla," said Kip. "Do you know anything about Tesla's assistants, specifically one he may have had around 1903?"

Garson shook his head. "No, assistants didn't get much notice unless they branched out on their own and made a name for themselves—like Tesla did. He worked for Edison for a time before setting up his own lab."

He regarded Kip curiously. "Why do you ask? What's this all about, Mr. Stevens?"

Kip hesitated. "Do you have time for a cup of coffee? I have a story to tell you that I think you'll find interesting. Maybe you can give me a different slant on it."

Dr. Garson looked at his watch. "I have a reception at four o'clock. I can spare an hour."

Over coffee in the student union, Kip told Garson the story of John and of his fixation with Tesla and the year 1903.

"As you can see, he does have some knowledge of physics," said Kip. "His psychiatrist thinks he's a history buff and is mistaking what he knows about the history of that time for memories."

"And you don't agree?"

"I'm not sure, but you tell me." Kip pulled out two enlarged photos from his bag and laid them in front of Garson.

"They are photos of the same man. I'm afraid I don't see the connection, Mr. Stevens."

"This is John, the man I found," said Kip, pointing to the picture on the left. "And this picture is of Tesla's assistant at a 1903 lecture in Slaterville."

Garson let an exclamation of surprise. "They look like the same man. You're certain this photo wasn't tampered with?"

"Very," replied Kip. "It's just as it appeared in the local paper in 1903. And the picture of John I took myself on my cell phone."

"Well, then, this man must be related to John."

"I thought so, too, but there is no record of Riley Harrington after that point in time and no record of any children." Kip quickly ran through the story of Harrington. "If he did, in fact, die in that grove in 1903, he can't be directly related to John."

"Unless Riley Harrington was a twin," said Garson. "Did you investigate that possibility?"

"No. I hadn't considered that," admitted Kip. "But I did check for siblings in the censuses and didn't find any."

"Many people had little means in those days, Mr. Stevens. It was not uncommon for twins to be separated at birth with one being given to a relative or placed in an orphanage."

"I supposed it could be a possibility," said Kip. "But there's something else." He recalled the weird electrical impulses in the Slaterville grove that he and Dr. Porter had experienced.

"The grove is where John claims he was shot," continued Kip. "This *is* where Harrington was shot. John now insists he's Riley Harrington—even under hypnosis."

Garson looked at Kip in astonishment. "How far away is this grove?"

"From here, about two hours."

"Can you take me there now?"

"What about your reception?"

"After what you have told me, the reception is not important."

CHAPTER SIXTEEN

A SHOCKING DISCOVERY

It was nearly dark when Kip drove into the old Slaterville grove.

"Show me the spot," said Garson as they got out of the car.

Kip grabbed a flashlight from the trunk and led Garson several feet into the orchard. He suddenly stopped. "Do you feel it?"

Garson nodded.

"Look at your watch," said Kip.

"It says 9 p.m.," reported Garson. "That's amazing."

Kip smiled. "It gets more amazing than that. Riley Harrington was shot around 8 p.m. in 1903—prior to the enactment of Daylight Savings Time.

"My God," murmured Garson.

As they moved closer to a tree, the electrical impulses became stronger; vibrations moved from their feet up through their legs.

"Are you certain there are no high voltage grids around here or buried wires?" asked Garson.

"The electric company says 'no,'" answered Kip.

"Where was Harrington shot?"

Kip pointed to an area. "Over there to the right of the tree."

"The trees nearest it are blighted," noted Garson as they approached the spot. "Direct your light here."

Garson pulled and scuffed at the illuminated patch of grass and weeds. Most of it was dead from the first frost of the fall season and came away easily. When it exposed charred earth, he pulled a dead branch from the tree and excitedly cleared away a wider area.

"My God," he murmured as more scorched earth became visible. He looked at Kip. "You said the drifters saw lightning bolts that night and the gates of hell opening to disappear Harrington."

"Yes."

Garson shook his head in awe. "I never thought to see the manifestation of one in my lifetime."

"What is it?" asked Kip.

"I think it's the mouth of one end of a wormhole."

Garson's declaration landed on Kip like a rock. It was one thing to accept something improbable in the theoretical. It was quite another to have an expert actually declare a physical manifestation of it. Kip wasn't ready to make that leap.

"It could also be the result of ball lightning," he said. "I checked it out. A description of it matches what the drifters saw that night."

"The description also matches what your man saw under hypnosis who now calls himself Riley Harrington and claims to have only memories of that time," Garson pointed out. "This is not the result of ball lightning. It's the origin of a time tunnel, Mr. Stevens, and I'll prove it to you. Take me to Fairfield where you found this man."

The sky was pitch black beneath a new moon when Kip pulled the car onto the shoulder of the road near Fairfield where he had found John. He barely brought the car to a stop before Garson threw open the door and jumped out.

"Do you have a shovel with you by any chance, Mr. Stevens?"

"I keep one in the trunk for snow," said Kip.

He got the shovel from the trunk and flashed his light on an area a few feet away. "The spot is over there."

Garson took the shovel from Kip and hurried over to the area. He quickly cleared away the brush. When he exposed the same scorched earth pattern as in the grove, he let out a hoot of excitement.

"This," he said without reservation, "is the other end of the wormhole."

Kip stared down at the ground, speechless.

Garson walked around the area. "Do you feel anything?" he asked.

"No," said Kip.

Garson frowned. "Neither do I. There doesn't appear to be any increased electromagnetic field here. Did you feel any impulses the night you found John similar to what you felt in the grove?"

"I don't know. I was too busy attending to him. I can't say for sure," answered Kip.

"Did the police investigating the scene mention any disturbances?" pressed Garson.

Kip shook his head. "None that I heard. Why?"

Garson's frown deepened. "It means the mouth has moved."

"Why—How?" Kip didn't know which question to ask first.

"A wormhole is not necessarily stationery," explained Garson. "When the storm ended, the electromagnetic field wasn't strong enough to hold it."

"Then why does the grove still vibrate with impulses?" quizzed Kip.

"The field must be stronger there," replied Garson. "Some areas of the world are known to exhibit stronger magnetic fields. The grove may be one of them and is holding the mouth of that end of the wormhole in place."

"So what does it mean, Professor?"

Garson was silent for a moment. "I don't know yet. Mr. Stevens, can you arrange for me to meet with John tomorrow?"

"Probably, but I wouldn't mention anything about wormholes to his psychiatrist," warned Kip. "She's resistant to anything that isn't scientifically rational."

Garson nodded. "I understand. I know the type well."

Kip dropped Dr. Garson off at his hotel and went on to the newspaper office to file his story on the science festival. It was well after midnight when he returned to his apartment.

His mind was still reeling. Wormholes…time tunnels…it was too incredulous to believe, but then who would have thought a hundred years ago there would be manned space flights to the moon?

* * * * *

Kip called Ericka to request the visit by Dr. Garson. He offered it as a casual suggestion—one physicist meeting another. She readily agreed to it, hoping that it would hold John in the present long enough for him to tap into and integrate memories of his real life.

Just before noon, Kip and Garson walked into the reception area of the psych unit of the hospital. Ericka arrived shortly after, and Kip made the introductions.

"I'm pleased to meet you," she said. "Thank you for coming, Dr. Garson."

Garson smiled. "The pleasure is all mine, Doctor."

"John is in the solarium. I'll take you there."

She led the way down a long hall to a large sunlit room where the patient awaited them.

"John, this is Dr. Garson, the physicist I told you about," she said.

"My name is Riley…Riley Harrington," he corrected her.

Ericka glanced uneasily at Kip and Garson, but the professor was unfazed. "I'm pleased to meet you, Riley. May we sit over there?"

Riley nodded, and Garson led him over to a couch. They sat down. Garson took out a pad and pencils and set them on the coffee table. Before long, both were writing out and conferring on mathematical formulas. Kip and Dr. Porter watched from across the room as John's interest and excitement increased with each exercise.

Ericka looked at Kip. "I'm afraid I have some bad news. John's injuries have healed and the hospital is releasing him."

"What about the amnesia?" asked Kip.

Ericka sighed. "Leanne and I tried to make the argument, but the executive board doesn't consider it an impediment to his ability to function on his own. I'll still continue to see him twice a month."

"Where will he live?" asked Kip, his brow knit in concern. "He has no money, no job."

"I know of a good homeless shelter. I can contact someone there," she offered.

Kip shook his head, vetoing the idea. "He would be too alone. He should be around someone who knows what he's going through."

Ericka glanced over at John. "Granted, but what's the alternative?"

"He can stay with me until he gets a job and adapts to his surroundings," replied Kip.

Ericka turned a concerning gaze on him. "Are you sure about that? You don't know who he really is, or what he was involved in to get those injuries. You could get pulled into something dangerous."

"I'll take the risk, Ericka. When can John leave?"

She paused with misgivings.

"I hope you know what you're doing, Kip. If John's agreeable to the arrangement, you can pick him up tomorrow. I have to go now. I have a patient to see."

As Ericka disappeared down the hall, Garson gathered together his papers and hurried over to Kip. "I can't believe it," he said, a look of wonder on his face. "I always knew it was theoretically possible, but scientists believed no one could survive such a journey with the radiation and intensity of the gravitational particles—"

"Dr. Garson, what are you talking about?"

"As incredible as this may seem, Mr. Stevens, I think this man is exactly who he says he is—Riley Harrington."

After last night's field trip, Kip should have been better prepared for Garson's pronouncement. He wasn't. To hear a noted physicist confirm such a possibility was unnerving to him. It violated his sense of reality. And it crossed his mind that maybe the professor was a little crazy, too.

"You said in your lecture that time travel isn't doable," he reminded Garson.

The physicist shrugged. "Apparently, I was wrong—along with the entire scientific community."

"How can you be so sure?" Kip demanded to know.

Garson's eyes twinkled. "He didn't know e=mc^2—Einstein's theory of relativity.

"All that proves is that John may not be a physicist," said Kip.

"On the contrary, he's a gifted physicist."

Kip puckered his brow in confusion. "How can you say that? You just said he didn't know the equation that is the cornerstone of modern physics."

"Einstein's theory of special relativity was published in 1905. His theory of general relativity wasn't published until 1916. If John is Riley Harrington, he wouldn't be familiar with either formula yet," explained Garson. "Neither does he know any of the modern theorists."

"Sorry, I need more than that, Professor."

Garson thought for a moment. "Do you have the 1903 photo that you showed me?"

"Yeah." Kip took it out of his computer bag.

"Look at the clothes Riley Harrington is wearing. Do they look like the same clothes John had on when you found him?" asked Garson.

Kip had been so shocked by the physical similarities between Riley and John he hadn't taken particular notice of the clothes.

He looked at the photo closely. "I don't know. Maybe. It's hard to tell. John wasn't wearing a coat—" He stopped as it suddenly came to him that Harrington's coat was found in the grove after he disappeared.

"If you check, I think you'll find that they are the same clothes," said Garson.

"I can't believe this," murmured Kip.

"Believe it, Mr. Stevens. We have before us a bona fide time traveler. And he must go back."

Kip raked a hand through his dark hair. He was coming around to accepting the possibility of reincarnation, but time travel?

"Jesus, I feel like I'm in a freakin' episode of the *Twilight Zone!*" he exploded.

Garson smiled. "I know how difficult this is to accept. Believe me, I'm having my own problems with it. And I know it's theoretically true. But Riley has to return to his own time. He came here by accident. Any distortion will create a ripple effect. By keeping him here, we could affect the past, present, and future in ways we can't begin to fathom."

Kip's head was spinning. "Where are you going to send him back to, Dr. Garson? There's no trace of him after 1903."

"You only checked the censuses in a few counties in New York and New Jersey, yes?"

Kip nodded.

"The country is a big place, Mr. Stevens. There were no social security numbers then. Nothing was computerized. It was easy to get lost."

"If he's so brilliant, wouldn't he have invented something and made a name for himself?" questioned Kip.

"Not necessarily," replied Garson. "Scientists build on the work of others. It was the time of the Industrial Revolution. Changes were happening rapidly. Ideas were stolen. Many didn't receive the recognition they should have had. It happens today."

Kip looked away for a moment, struggling to put some order to his thoughts.

"Okay, let's suppose you're right, Professor, that John—Riley—is a time traveler. He has seen the future. He knows what's possible now. If you send him back, he'll most assuredly affect the future."

"There are people who believe that da Vinci and Tesla were given a vision of the future," replied Garson. "Like them, Riley might be able to draw, design, create mathematical equations for what he's seen here, but there won't be the means to execute them. The materials won't exist yet in his time. So, like da Vinci and Tesla, he'll probably be considered a visionary…. But it wouldn't hurt to limit his exposure by containing his environment," added the professor.

"How the hell are you going to send him back?!" Kip demanded to know.

Garson shook his head. "I can't say yet. But first things first, we have to find the mouth of the wormhole on this end….Wormholes don't usually move that fast," he said, thinking aloud. "It can't be far away."

He looked at Kip. "If you remember my lecture, the openings will be close together in location…"

The rest of the professor's musings were lost to Kip as he felt himself slipping beneath the water in a sea of the bizarre.

Garson smiled, the vacant expression on the reporter's face telling. "I thought reporters were truth seekers, Mr. Stevens."

Kip refocused his attention on the professor. "What?"

"I thought reporters were truth seekers," repeated Garson.

Kip was silent for a moment. "What is truth, Professor?"

Garson smiled again. "Ah, the age-old debate, the answer problematic because truth is selective to people. To many, it is whatever the mind is willing or wanting to accept. The true seeker of truth never discounts anything however much it strains credulity and violates his sense of reality."

Maddie Claymore jumped to Kip's mind. She had told him much the same thing. He gave a satirical laugh. "And what is reality?"

"Another hotly debated question, for a different time," responded Garson. "Broadly speaking, it's everything you perceive tangible and intangible, which means it's always subject to change."

"And how does one deal with a 'change' that unravels everything he thought he knew about his world, Professor?"

"With rationality," answered Garson. "Mankind is only at the threshold of comprehending the complexities of the universe. That's what science is all about…discovering possibilities and making them possible. Who could have imagined the breadth of space exploration 50 years ago?"

"Yes, I've been trying to keep that in mind," responded Kip brusquely. He took a deep breath. "So, what's the next step?"

"When is Riley Harrington due to be released from the hospital?" asked Garson. "We'll require his cooperation."

Riley Harrington…Kip didn't know if he could get use to calling John by that name. "The hospital is kicking him loose tomorrow," he replied. "If he's agreeable, he'll be staying with me."

"Excellent. I'm going back to the university. I have a lot of work to do."

"I'll drive you," offered Kip.

Garson shook his head. "I'll take a cab to a car rental place. You have other things to do. You mentioned a diary. See if it can give us a clue or a key as to a window of time."

"What do you mean by window of time?" asked Kip.

"We have to try to return Riley as close to the time of his leaving as we can. He won't have aged, but everyone else will be older, including Elizabeth," explained Garson. "And Riley can't be allowed to affect the history already written."

"Right—the ripple effect," remarked Kip flippantly.

"This is important, Mr. Stevens—"

"Kip…call me Kip."

"Very good. I'm David," said Garson. "We need to know the earliest point we can strategically shoot for, Kip, or Riley may end up in Slaterville 50 years later."

Kip dropped Dr. Garson off at the rental car facility.

A part of him stubbornly refused to buy into the professor's theory without more proof, and he headed to the police station. When he entered the building, he met Detective Gillespie on his way out.

"If you're here to see me, Stevens, it'll have to wait."

"No, I came to see Peg. Is she here?"

"She's in the lab."

Kip made his way to the third-floor forensics lab. An attractive woman in her mid-thirties, off-beat with purplish red hair and pink cat-eyeglasses, looked up from her microscope and smiled. "You still around, Stevens? The bet in the office was you wouldn't last a year here."

Kip raised a brow at the idea that he was the subject of an office pool. "Maybe I like the peace and quiet of a small town."

Peg looked at him, skeptical. "Yeah, sure you do. The word is that you stepped on an important political donor's toes and got canned by your paper. Is that true?"

Kip shrugged. "The truth hurts. The newspaper gave me a choice of making a public apology and retracting my story or finding employment elsewhere. I chose the latter. It's as simple as that."

"A good looking, big city guy like you…nothing is as simple as that. Be forewarned, Stevens. This is a small town. Your secret will come out."

Kip laughed. "Well, you're all going to be disappointed. I'm just an ordinary guy who needed a break from hypocrisy."

"Ha! Don't think you're going to get that here, honey. What do you need?"

"I want to see John Doe's clothes," said Kip.

"They're in the evidence room and the case is still open. You know that's against procedure, right?"

Kip nodded. "I just need a quick look."

Peg hesitated. "Since Hank hasn't been able to determine if the guy has committed a crime yet, I'll call down and tell Frank to let you see the box."

"Thanks, Peg. I owe you."

"Yeah, yeah. I'm still waiting for that lunch, Stevens."

"I'm good for it."

"Damn straight, you are."

When Kip arrived at the evidence room, the clerk was carrying out the box. "Sign here and remain in plain sight," he said. "And don't open anything that is sealed in a plastic bag."

Kip carried the box to a table. The shirt and vest were sealed. He laid out the pants and shoes and pulled out his 1903 newspaper photo of Riley Harrington.

"Frank, do you have a magnifying glass?" he asked.

The clerk rummaged around in a drawer and pulled out one like a kid might find as a toy in a Cracker Jack's box.

Kip looked at him with a crooked smile. "Really?"

The clerk shrugged. "It's all I got."

"Must be the budget cuts," quipped Kip, taking the item.

Making do with it, he compared the trousers on the table with the pants in the photo. The photo was old, but the detail was sharp enough for him to make out that the tweed and style looked similar enough. Still, it was not conclusive enough for his skeptical side.

The man in the photo wore leather spats over his shoes. Kip searched the evidence box. Spats lay at the bottom. His heart beat a rapid tattoo against his chest.

When Gillespie returned to the station, Kip was waiting for him.

The detective let out a groan. "You still here? What is it now? I'm busy."

"Did you check out the grove in Slaterville?" asked Kip.

"Yeah." Gillespie's brows dipped into a frown. "You know that place feels really weird."

Kip smothered a smile. "What did you find?"

"Not much. Just that the soil samples taken from there match some dirt that was on John Doe's shoes," replied the detective. "All it proves is that he was in the grove prior to being dumped along the side of the road. There's nothing to say that he was shot there, but the Slaterville police are checking out the possibility."

"You have a friend on the Slaterville Police Department, don't you?" queried Kip.

"I wouldn't call him a friend…more like a friendly point of contact." Gillespie's eyes narrowed in suspicion. "Why do you want to know?"

"I need you to call him and ask if there is still an evidence box for a man named Riley Harrington," said Kip. "The date is November 1, 1903."

"Why do you want to know about a case from 1903?" quizzed Gillespie.

"It's for a story I'm working on, Hank."

The detective turned a curious eye on Kip. "Does it have anything to do with this John Doe case?"

"Why would you think that?" asked Kip.

"Well, gee, I don't know. Maybe because John Doe was shot with a gun made in 1900, and he was found dressed in clothes from that era," replied Gillespie with heavy sarcasm. "You tell me."

Kip smiled. "What…you think John is a time traveler?"

A look of panic crossed Gillespie's face, and he glanced around to see if anyone had overheard. "Now, did I say that? Geez, keep your voice down, Stevens. That's how crazy rumors get started, and I'm up for promotion."

Kip leaned in and whispered. "What's the connection, then?"

"How the hell do I know!" exclaimed the detective. "You're the one who said there was one."

"I didn't say that. You did."

"Damn it, Stevens! Talking with you is like talking in circles."

Kip laughed. "Are you going to make the call?"

"Yeah, yeah. Then get the hell out of here so I can get some work done."

"The case is closed. You'll need to set me up with an appointment to go through the contents if there is a box," said Kip.

Gillespie glared at him as he picked up the phone and placed the call to the Slaterville Police Department.

"Well?" asked Kip, when the detective hung up.

"They're checking. Sgt. Zimmerman will call me. I'll let you know."

Kip left the police station and headed for the newspaper office. He was nearly there when he received the call from Gillespie with the news he was hoping for, and he turned the car around and headed for Slaterville.

* * * * *

The evidence room was cold, dark, and dreary with no windows. It looked similar to the one in Fairfield.

The clerk handed him the box. "Don't know why you're interested in this old case," he commented. "It was closed. You're lucky it's still here. Police departments don't usually keep an evidence box on closed cases this long."

"Yeah, I know. Thanks," said Kip.

He carried the box over to a table. The contents could either be proof of an implausible truth that the world might not be ready to accept or a big disappointment, and he wasn't sure which he wanted it to be. He hesitated a moment, then tore off the dusty lid. The box smelled musty inside.

Luckily, there was no sealed evidence. Kip lifted out the coat, and he felt his heart skip a beat. The article of clothing was John's size—and there was a dark stain that he assumed was blood and a bullet hole in the area where John had been shot. What's more, the material and the tweed on the coat seemed to match that of the trousers and vest John was found wearing.

Kip took out his pen knife and cut a small square of material from an inconspicuous place inside the coat. When he looked into the box again, he sucked in his breath. There lay the gun.

"Has anybody asked to see this box in the last three weeks?" he asked.

The clerk looked at the sign-in sheet. "No."

"How far back do your log-in sheets go?"

"Depends on the case...usually 10 years," replied the clerk. "That's when evidence is destroyed in a closed case. How far back are you lookin' to go?"

"I'd like to know that this box hasn't been opened since 1903."

The clerk looked at Kip in surprise. "Sorry, can't help you there, but by the looks of it and location of it in the storage area, that box hasn't been opened in a lot of years.

Kip thought for a moment. "Is there a chance that someone could have come in and removed something and put it back without you knowing?"

"Like what?" asked the clerk, somewhat affronted.

"Like the gun," said Kip.

"Why would anybody want to do that?"

"Maybe to commit a crime and confuse the police. It isn't unheard of for a gun to disappear from an evidence room and be used in a crime," replied Kip. "A cold case box would be a great place to hide a murder weapon. Is there any way to tell if this gun has been fired recently?"

"Only an expert could tell you that." The clerk regarded Kip with annoyance. "Look, Mr. Stevens, I don't know what your interest in this is or what you're trying to prove, but I know my job, and I'm tellin' you no one has accessed that box in a helluva lot of years. The dust hasn't even been disturbed."

Kip had to admit the clerk had a point.

CHAPTER SEVENTEEN

FURTHER EVIDENCE OF WHAT?

Gillespie stared at Kip as though he had grown two heads. "You want me to do what?!"

"I want you to request a ballistics test on the gun in the 1903 Slaterville case and compare the bullet to the one the doctor took out of John," repeated Kip.

"Why should I do that?"

"Humor me."

"I'm humoring you now by not having you thrown out of the station with such a harebrained request," blustered Gillespie. "You're telling me you think John was shot with a gun that was used in an apparent homicide over a century ago. Do you know how nuts that sounds?"

"Trust me, Gillespie, I do. But I have reason to believe it may be the case."

"What reason?"

"It's a lead I'm following up. You know my motto…no stone unturned."

The detective snorted. "This isn't a stone; it's a pebble. You've got to give me more than that. Zimmerman and the brass will think I'm certifiable, and you know I'm up for a promotion. I'm not sticking my neck out just so you have a story to write."

"Look, Hank. It isn't a stretch of the imagination for a dirty cop to steal a gun out of evidence, commit a crime with it, and put it back," argued Kip. "Think about it. No one is going to check there for the weapon. And evidence goes missing all the time."

Gillespie had to admit Kip had a point. "Dammit, Stevens! Why can't you make my life easier and move back to Philadelphia?"

Kip grinned. "You would miss me. How long will it take for you to get the report?"

"I didn't say I would do it, Stevens. If I did, it would probably take a month or more to get the results. The state and FBI labs are always backed up, and this isn't exactly a priority."

"I can't wait that long, Hank. I need the results in 24 hours. How about a private lab?"

"Private labs cost money, and their findings may not stand up in court."

Kip ran a hand through his dark hair in frustration. Another wall.

"Look, I'll pay the costs," he said. "If the bullets match and the court refuses to accept the findings once you do have a case, you can send it to the FBI lab for verification."

"Why in such a hurry?"

"I have a deadline."

As Gillespie continued to mull over the proposition, Kip groaned. "Come on, Hank. It's a simple ballistics test. You can't lose. If there isn't a match, I'm the one out the money. If there is one, you could be a hero…maybe even featured on one of those TV reality cop shows."

A gleam came into the detective's eye and a smile hovered around his mouth as he considered the possibility.

"Might help with that promotion," Kip added.

"I'll consider it and that's all I'm promising," said the detective. "Now get out of here before I have you thrown out."

"Okay, okay, I'm leaving. Just one more thing." He produced the piece of material he had cut from Harrington's coat. "Ask Peg if this is a match to John's pants and vest."

Gillespie raised his arm and pointed to the door. "Out, Stevens! This isn't your private lab."

Kip set the swatch on the desk and winked. "Call me when you have the reports."

"You got peanut butter in your ears? I said I would consider it. Out!" yelled the detective.

Kip chuckled as he left the floor.

CHAPTER EIGHTEEN

WHAT IS REALITY?

"Hey, Gillespie, there's a call for you from some lab," yelled a fellow detective.

Gillespie hurried over to his desk and picked up the phone. "Detective Gillespie here."

As the caller imparted his news, the detective's face registered astonishment. When he hung up, he dropped into his chair. "Get Kip Stevens' ass in here. Pronto!" he bellowed to a passing officer.

When Kip got the summons, he didn't have to ask "why." And on his way to the police station, he tried to figure out what his response should be. Gillespie was going to demand answers—answers Kip was still grappling with himself. Their reality was a world of the five senses. How the hell was he going to explain to someone like Gillespie a reality based upon quantum physics? Even someone as intelligent and scientifically minded as Dr. Porter refused to embrace it.

Kip walked into the police station and took the stairs two at a time to the second floor. Gillespie didn't look to be in a good mood, and he approached the detective's desk with a slower step.

"You wanted to see me, Hank?"

Gillespie looked up at Kip and tapped the file in front of him. "This is the ballistics report you wanted. Do you know what it says?"

"I have a pretty good idea," admitted Kip.

"What else did your source tell you?" the detective demanded to know. "Who the hell is this John Doe?! On paper, they guy doesn't seem to exist!"

"Calm down, Hank. I was acting on a hunch."

"Yesterday, you said it was a lead. Give me something, Stevens, or I swear I'll lock you up for withholding evidence."

Kip thought fast. "Would you believe the psychic gave me the lead that eventually led to the hunch?"

The detective stared at Kip, the wind taken out of his sails. He couldn't disparage the woman's credentials when his own police department had used her to a good end.

"Are you bullshittin' me, Stevens?"

Kip raised his hands. "No, I swear it."

"What else do you know about this case?"

"I'm as confused as you are," Kip answered honestly.

"Does this guy remember anything yet?" pressed Gillespie.

"Uh, nothing that would satisfy your case. Maybe we should just assume that it was a bizarre accident that occurred during the Slaterville Founders' Day Celebration," suggested Kip.

The detective glanced down at the report on his desk. "No, removing that gun from the evidence room and returning it shows planning and premeditation."

"I wouldn't read too much into it," said Kip.

Gillespie looked at him in surprise. "Two days ago, you were in a lather to get this ballistics test. Now that it has been proven two men were shot with the same gun over a hundred years apart, you tell me not to read too much into it. What the hell is wrong with you?"

"It could be something as simple as a cuckolded husband wanting to dispense some poetic justice," replied Kip, in an effort to divert the detective's focus.

Gillespie ignored him. "It would have to be a cop," he continued to muse. "Only a cop would know about that gun and be able to get in and out of the evidence room unnoticed. What was this John Doe into?"

"Why don't you ask the psychic?" interjected Kip.

Gillespie glared at him. "Get out of here, Stevens, but stay close. I'm not convinced that you're telling me everything you know. By the way, that piece of fabric you left behind…Peg said it was a match to John Doe's clothes. Where did it come from?"

"From a coat in the Slaterville evidence box," said Kip.

"John Doe's coat was in a 1903 evidence box!" exclaimed Gillespie.

Kip immediately regretted disclosing the information. How was he going to explain this one?

Luckily, the detective came up with his own explanation. "Holy cripes! Someone faked an evidence box!" he exclaimed. "This is big. Get out, Stevens. I have to think."

Kip didn't have to be told twice and hurried out of the police station. He just hoped Gillespie would follow his theory far enough down that rabbit hole to buy Riley and Professor Garson some time.

As Kip drove to his office, he was not feeling so blasé about the results of the ballistics tests and the match of the material. The last leg of the stool had been kicked out from under any chance for a practical answer. The findings should have surprised, maybe even shocked him. Instead, he felt numb.

There was no retreating to the world he had known. It didn't exist anymore. It wasn't that it had been perfect. Far from it. But there was the kind of comfort there that one found in ignorance. And he had to ask himself. Was he really a truth seeker? More to the point, faced with his first real test, did he actually want to be one, for he had learned there were simple truths, and there were mind-blowing truths that transcended the rules of one's construct of what was real.

Maddie Claymore came to mind again. She had told him that he would have to straddle two worlds—the world of belief and the world of disbelief. He jammed on his brakes at the red light with a sudden epiphany. She knew!

He had thought her confused at the nursing home when she had identified John as Riley, but she knew they were one and the same. How? How could she have known?

Car horns began to beep, and Kip realized the light had turned green. He immediately changed course and turned down the side street to his favorite drinking hole.

It was 3:30 in the afternoon. The place was fairly empty, and he took his usual seat at the bar. "Jerry, give me a double Scotch."

The bartender set the drink on the bar and looked at Kip curiously as the reporter threw back half the contents in a single gulp.

"A little early for you, isn't it, Stevens? What happened? Did a girl finally see through your charm?"

"Funny, McGinty."

Kip moodily twirled the glass in his hands. "Do you believe in co-incidence or that things happen for a reason, Jerry?"

The bartender shrugged. "I don't know. I never really thought about it."

"Neither did I until now."

Kip gulped the rest of his drink and ordered another.

By the time he walked into the newsroom, he was in no mood to be trifled with. When the assistant editor approached him, the man drew back at the black look Kip gave him and dropped the assignment on the desk without the usual commentary.

Kip picked up the sheet and read through the notes. He was to cover a political event. It was a coveted assignment for him; he loved the theater of the absurd. But after the last few days, it seemed trivial.

He walked into Dittmore's office and tossed the assignment sheet on the desk. "I can't do this," he said.

Dittmore looked up in surprise. "What do you mean you can't do it? It's red meat to you." The editor's eyes narrowed. "Have you been drinking?"

Kip collapsed into a chair. "Yes."

Dittmore regarded him with concern. His star reporter was as clear-headed as they came. Now he was drinking in the afternoon and refusing a plum assignment?

"What the hell is going on with you, Stevens?"

Kip ran a hand wearily across his face. "Did you know that there are realities you can't touch or smell or see or hear? They exist only in a damned equation."

Now the editor was alarmed. "I don't know what's bothering you but take some time off and get a handle on it," he ordered. "Don't come back until you do."

CHAPTER NINETEEN

SCIENCE FICTION?

While Kip was still grappling with the idea of time travel being real, he was surprised how easily John accepted it as fact. Perhaps because he was a physicist. And perhaps, thought Kip ironically, the nonsensical was the only thing that made sense right now.

As he drove John to his apartment, Kip could see that John viewed his surroundings through the lens of a scientist seeing the marvel of discovery for the first time, but he felt no connection to this world as a participant, and no amount of therapy was going to change that, concluded Kip. He was just going to have to accept that John was who he said he was—Riley Harrington—a man from another time.

Kip pulled into the three-story building's parking lot. They got out of the car and climbed the stairs to the second floor.

"It isn't fancy, but it's home," said Kip, opening the door to his apartment.

Riley entered and slowly walked through the rooms. It was a typical bachelor's pad furnished with the bare necessities. Riley found the plumbing in the bathroom and the appliances in the kitchen of particular interest.

"Alternating current, as in the hospital," he noted with approval. "It is gratifying to know that all these years later Mr. Tesla continues to win the day against Mr. Edison and his direct current."

"Actually, we make use of direct current as well now—in our industries," said Kip.

Riley looked at him in surprise. "How is that? It does not travel long distances, and it is not easy or economical to switch from high to low voltage."

"We have other ways of transmitting high voltage current now."

"Interesting," murmured Riley.

Kip pointed to the couch. "It pulls out into a bed. You can sleep there."

He looked at the jeans, pullover shirt, and jacket that he had given Riley to wear. They were a little big on him. "Tomorrow we'll see about getting some other clothes for you."

"I'm going to need my own clothes returned," Riley reminded him.

"Oh, right," said Kip. "I guess you can't return to 1903 in twenty-first century garb. The police will want to keep your clothes until the case is closed. Maybe we can find something suitable in a costume or vintage shop."

Riley nodded. "I'm sorry, Kip. I know this isn't easy for you."

"It can't be easy for you either," responded Kip.

"It's not so difficult when you come from the world of science."

"How will you use all the knowledge you now have of the future?"

Riley smiled. "Mr. Tesla had his peculiarities. But he was a brilliant man. All the things I have seen, he already imagined. And he was thought to be a strange man. All men of vision are when their intellect exceeds the boundaries of their time."

Riley frowned. "Because of this, I have read in your book that he was not given the credit he deserves. Others later took it using his patents, some for the greater good, others purely for profit. It was never about money for Mr. Tesla, Kip. It was about the advancement of all mankind. I shall endeavor to carry forth his banner."

Kip regarded Riley. "I believe that you will, but you will be happy to know that Mr. Tesla is now getting the recognition due him…. Just out of curiosity, did Dr. Porter ever give you back the book I brought for you on Tesla?"

"Yes. I think she has given up trying to shock me into this century," replied Riley.

Kip chuckled. "You really have shaken her confidence as a psychiatrist, you know."

Riley smiled apologetically. "Indeed, and I am sorry about that."

"She's more or less convinced you're pulling a scam you know."

Riley nodded. "Perhaps one day she can hear the truth."

Kip gave him a wry smile. "I doubt that. Well, you must be hungry. I'll rustle up something for us to eat. You can read the paper or watch TV."

Riley wrinkled his brow in confusion. "TV?"

"Television—over there." Kip pointed to the 52" flat screen hanging on the wall.

He picked up the remote and turned it on. When a picture appeared, Riley moved closer, mesmerized by the moving and talking images.

"A Russian scientist, Constantin Perskyi, read a paper to the International Electricity Congress at the International World's Fair in Paris in 1900. He talked about the work of others in the field of electromechanical technologies. Perskyi called it television, but I don't think he imagined anything such as this. How is this possible?"

Kip shrugged. "Circuit boards and something called cable network. I'm a journalist, not an engineer. All I care about is that the thing comes on when I click the button on this remote. It's one of the wonders of the modern world. There are many others that aren't so great," he added wryly.

He handed the remote to Riley and showed him how to change the channels. "It's wireless. It operates with batteries and uses something called infrared light. Infrared light is—"

"I know what infrared light is," said Riley. "It was discovered in 1800 by an astronomer named William Herschel, and the technology has been adapted for use in the Nernst lamps."

"Sorry," said Kip. "I guess that we, in this modern world, tend to assume science is our invention."

Riley smiled. "The term 'modern' can be subjective." He studied the remote in his hand, somewhat perplexed. "I know what batteries are as well, but they are much too large to fit this."

Kip opened the back of the remote and showed Riley much smaller batteries. "These are AA batteries." He held out his arm. "My watch uses a battery smaller than the size of my fingertip."

"Interesting," murmured Riley.

Kip left Riley playing with the remote and examining the batteries while he went into the kitchen to stir up some food. If a television could blow Riley's mind, Kip wondered what a computer and the internet would do—not to mention the concept of social media.

After dinner, Kip put the dishes in a dishwasher, once again amazing Riley at the extent of modern technology. When Riley fell asleep on the pullout couch, Kip went to his room and took out Julia Trowbridge's diary. He hadn't shown it to Riley. Parts of it would probably upset him.

Kip settled himself comfortably in bed and began to read through the entries with closer attention. Partway he stopped to rub his temples. At the finish, he could find nothing that would indicate a window of time obscure or otherwise.

Kip didn't sleep much that night and was up early the next morning. Following Dr. Garson's advice to limit Riley's exposure to the modern world, Kip whipped up a breakfast of eggs, bacon, toast and coffee, instead of going out to a restaurant. Still, Riley found much to be amazed about in Kip's small apartment, and he was full of questions.

"What kind of town was Slaterville in 1903?" asked Kip, when he had satisfied enough of Riley's curiosity.

Riley was thoughtful for a moment. "It seems progressive and prosperous. But lumber is the chief industry. It's never wise to put all your eggs in one basket as they say."

Kip caught Riley's continual lapse into the use of the present tense when he spoke of that time and was struck once again by the "Twilight Zone" effect to everything.

"Is there anything that stands out to you about the town, an event, a person?" questioned Kip.

Riley shook his head. "Except for Elizabeth, I don't recall anything of note. Why?"

"Dr. Garson is trying to pinpoint a window of time to which you will return."

"What do you mean?" asked Riley.

"Garson said he can't send you back to 1903," replied Kip.

Riley looked at him in alarm. "But I need to return to 1903!"

"Garson said you can't go back before the creation of the time tunnel, and he doesn't know when that occurred," explained Kip.

Riley raked a hand through his hair, agitated. "I don't understand. It was obviously there in November of 1903."

"I know. Look, I'm no physicist, but as I understand it, if you go back before you were shot, that drifter could shoot you again, this time killing you," said Kip. "If you go back just after being shot, as seriously wounded as you were, you might not survive your injuries.

"Besides that, time travel isn't an exact science for us yet," Kip pointed out dryly. "Assuming that the professor can send you back, he's trying to determine a safe point that won't create some kind of inconsistency in history. Does this make sense to you?"

Riley nodded. "A man named H.G. Wells wrote a book called *The Time Machine* that inspired much debate among my colleagues on the topic of paradoxes."

Just then, the phone rang. Riley watched in fascination as Kip picked up a small, thin, rectangular box, slid a finger across the face of it, and put it up to his ear. Riley's eyes widened in further amazement as Kip held a quick conversation on it.

When Kip ended the call, he noticed the wonder on Riley's face. "It's called an iPhone—a telephone," he said.

"But how can that be?" asked Riley. "There is no box, no speaking piece. It is not connected to anything."

Kip explained the rudiments of how it worked and how it plugged into a charger to repower. He decided it was best not to show Riley all the things the invention could do. The young scientist's mind was already blown by just the telephone feature.

"By the way, that was David who called," said Kip. "He's coming by in an hour. He thinks he has found something."

When Garson arrived, he spread out papers on the kitchen table, his excitement palpable. "Look at this. We are several years into a sunspot cycle."

At the look of confusion on Kip's and Riley's faces, he slowed down to explain. "It's a 22-year-phenomenon. It occurs when the poles of the sun flip every 11 years, then flip back for another 11 years. But what's important is that the cycle is currently at solar maximum."

"I still don't get it," said Kip.

"It means more intense solar storms impacting Earth's electromagnetic fields," replied Garson.

He shuffled through the papers and came up with a chart. "See this," he said, pointing to a line. "This shows that a measurable solar storm occurred on October 31 through November 1 of 1903. The current followed the 105th meridian from the North Pole through Canada to the United States, then radiated east and west.

"According to newspapers," he continued, "it affected electrical machinery and instruments in nearly every part of the country. Some parts of the country experienced two such storms a few hours apart. You should have been able to see an aurora borealis where you were, Riley."

Riley nodded. "Yes, I remember. It was most impressive."

"An old man I had spoken with in Slaterville mentioned there had been a solar storm at that time," recalled Kip.

"Ah, I understand now," said Riley.

Kip gave a snort of impatience. "Well, I don't. Would someone please explain it to me?"

"That's how I ended up here," said Riley. "The storm on November 1, 1903, was occurring at the same time as the storm here."

Garson nodded. "They just had to overlap for a short period of time."

Kip shook his head, incredulous. "So all of this is because two solar storms occurred at the same time over a hundred years apart. What are the chances of that happening?"

"Actually, not as remote as they may seem," said Garson. "I discovered that the solar cycle in the early twentieth century—number 14—mirrors the solar cycle we are in today. I believe the solar storms are the key to returning Riley to his own time period."

"How? How do you do that?" Kip demanded to know, exasperation creeping into his tone.

"We have to figure out when the next corresponding storms occur that have the strength to activate the mouths of the wormhole at the same time," replied Garson.

"Sounds simple to me," remarked Kip flippantly.

"It's not so daunting, Kip. At solar maximum, an average of 20 solar flares can occur per day. Solar flares have a classification of C, M, or X with C being the weakest and X the strongest," explained Garson. "NOAA spotted two flares today in the M class and C class. Stronger flares are expected in the coming months. It's only a matter of time until an Earth-directed coronal mass ejection occurs strong enough to trigger the mouth of the wormhole to open here."

"What about the other end of the wormhole in Slaterville?" asked Kip.

Garson pulled out a chart from among the papers on the table. "I discovered that a sizable geomagnetic storm hit Earth on this side December 1, 1907."

Riley looked at him, visibly upset. "You are saying I cannot return to a year before 1907?"

"I don't know that for certain," replied Garson. "The grove is highly charged. It wouldn't take too strong a storm to open the mouth of the wormhole there, so it's possible there were other storms in between 1903 and 1907 that went unnoticed. There wasn't any electricity or phone service in rural areas like Slaterville to disrupt then," he pointed out. "Unless people saw a borealis, they might not have known a storm had occurred."

"Thomas Marshall lost his money in the Panic of 1907," recalled Kip. "The men convicted of killing Riley were released near the end of that year. It can't be a coincidence that so many things happened around the same time then."

"Who was Thomas Marshall?" asked Garson.

"Elizabeth Slater's husband."

Kip immediately realized his slip of the tongue when he saw shock and disbelief scroll across Riley's face.

"Oh, geez, I'm sorry, Riley. I wasn't thinking—"

"She married him?! When? When did she marry him?" Riley demanded to know.

"1904," replied Kip.

"How do you know this?"

Kip hesitated, knowing where this would lead. "I-uh-read it in Julia Trowbridge's diary."

Riley looked at him in surprise. "Julia had a diary?"

Kip nodded. "Her granddaughter gave it to me."

"What else does the diary say?"

"Riley, maybe Dr. Porter should be here—"

"Kip, what else does the diary say?!"

"She wasn't happy in the marriage," said Kip.

Riley fixed a sharp eye on him. "There's something you're not telling me. What is it?"

Kip hesitated again. "The diary ends in December 1907. I could find no record of Elizbeth after that point."

Riley looked at him in alarm. "Did Elizabeth die?"

"I don't know," said Kip. "A fire destroyed a lot of the records."

"Oh, my God!" he cried.

"Riley, it doesn't necessarily mean she died," Kip tried to assure him. "The historian said that women in that time were largely forgotten. History focused on prominent men who built the town."

Riley wasn't mollified. "Dr. Garson, I have to go back either before Elizabeth marries Marshall or before she disappears."

Garson scratched his head. "That's a tall order. I would have to know more information."

"Maybe she divorced her husband and left town," suggested Kip.

"Is there a record of a divorce?" questioned Riley.

Kip shook his head.

Harrington fixed a piercing gaze on him. "Have you told us everything that is in the diary?"

Kip shifted uneasily. He could feel Dr. Porter sitting on his shoulder scolding him for opening that door. Now, he had no choice but to walk through it.

"There was something more," he admitted. "When Marshall lost his money, he pressured Elizabeth to give him control of her trust fund. When she refused, he threatened to have her committed to a mental institution."

A heavy pall fell over the room.

"Were you able to find any record of Elizabeth being committed to a mental hospital?" asked Riley.

Again, Kip shook his head. "There were only a couple of asylums and sanitariums within a 100-mile radius at the time. None of them had any record of Elizabeth Marshall."

Riley turned away. "Then I have to assume the worst…that she died," he said, his voice choking with emotion.

"Not necessarily. Her husband could have committed her under a pseudonym to protect the family name," interjected Garson.

Riley turned back sharply. "Do you have any idea what those places were like then? I would be more solaced to know that Elizabeth died a quick death. You have to get me back, David, before it is too late."

Garson and Kip glanced at each other.

"Your move, Doc."

Garson took a deep breath and thought for a moment.

"When did the Panic of 1907 begin?" he asked.

Kip took out his computer and googled it.

"It started October 14th with the collapse of the options market," he reported. "Shock waves continued in the market as major New York banks failed throughout November and December, triggering a run on banks throughout the country for the next couple of years. Marshall probably lost his money sometime between the end of October and end of November of that year."

"If the solar storm occurred December 1st in 1907, then I may return in time to save Elizabeth," said Riley with renewed hope. "It should give us enough time to find the opening of the wormhole here."

"I'm afraid it isn't that easy," cautioned Garson.

"Why not?" demanded Kip, tiring of all the curve balls.

"There's something called the space-time continuum," explained Garson. "The time is different there. It won't correspond with our time here. We have to find out what the date is there to know if the 1907 storm is our corresponding storm."

Riley looked at Garson in alarm. "Are you saying December 1st may have passed…that we may have missed that storm?"

"I'm sorry, but, yes, it's a good possibility."

"So Riley is just as likely to end up in time anywhere between 1907 and now," observed Kip.

Garson nodded. "Regretfully, I'm afraid so."

"What matters the year if Elizabeth is not present? Without her, there is no life for me in any time," said Riley, disheartened.

"Come on, Doc. Your quantum formulas and charts must be able to give you something more definitive," insisted Kip.

Garson kneaded his forehead trying to think. Suddenly, his features brightened. "I think I know of a way we can pinpoint the year there."

Riley's spirits rose. "What is it?"

"We can ask Elizabeth—if she's still there. We can establish a cosmic link."

Silence followed as Kip and Riley stared at him as though the physicist had lost his mind.

Riley walked away visibly upset.

"Not funny, Doc," said Kip.

"I'm not joking," responded Garson. "The body is 60% water and contains many salts. This makes it a good conductor of electric current. Where there is an electric current there is a magnetic field."

Again, he was met with silence.

"It's not science fiction," he insisted. "Every cell, every organ and the brain are all electromagnetic fields working in synchronization. We are all cosmic beings connected to the universe and each other through electromagnetic fields—including our minds."

Kip shook his head, frustration bordering on anger. "I went along with the other stuff, Doc, but cosmic links are where I draw the line."

"Gentlemen, just hear me out," pleaded Garson. "Riley, how emotionally and physically connected are you and Elizabeth?"

Riley returned to the table. "We have known each other for only a short time, but I dare say that we share a deep affection."

"They were planning to elope, David. How much more connected do they have to be?" interjected Kip dryly.

Garson ignored him. "Riley, may I assume that you have held her hand and kissed her?"

Riley balked. "David, I really don't wish to discuss such a private matter."

"That's all I need to know," said Garson. "In 2007, a Harvard Medical School psychiatrist suggested a 'physiological concordance' or phase locking entanglement between two people through their emotional and physical interactions. A later study determined that two people can become physiologically in tune with each other without needing to have physical contact if a connection has already been made."

"You are saying that I may be able to connect with Elizabeth mentally if we have made a prior emotional or physical connection," clarified Riley.

Garson nodded. "The stronger the better."

"It's fantasy," scoffed Kip.

"No, my skeptical friend, it's science," countered Garson. "We call it quantum entanglement."

Kip gave a short laugh. "I call it absurd."

Riley looked at him. "It's absurd that I'm here in the first place, Kip, and yet here I am. I will consider any remedy to the situation, however strange it may sound or implausible it may seem."

"Perhaps we should take a break," suggested Garson, feeling the tenseness in the room.

"No, proceed," said Riley. "I fail to understand how this enables me to communicate with Elizabeth."

"Well, every thought, every word spoken, every emotion we have goes out into the universe as a wave," explained Garson. "We just have to connect her wave with yours."

Kip snorted. "If that's the case, there are a helluva lot of waves out there. How are you going to find the right ones—with some mathematical formula?" he questioned with sarcasm.

Garson gave him a smile of forbearance. "No, with meditation. When someone has strong emotions, it creates a vibration. The deeper the emotion and the more consuming the thoughts, the greater the vibration."

"So, to connect with Elizabeth all that is required of me is to meditate," reiterated Riley.

"The Russians and the CIA tried this mind melding stuff from the 1970's into the 1990's. It didn't work," said Kip.

"How do you know it didn't work?" questioned Garson. "Because the government said so?"

"Do you know otherwise, Doc?"

"I don't know anything for certain, but if the program was so unsuccessful why did it take the CIA 20 years to shut it down? Or did they really shut it down?"

Kip didn't have an answer. "The idea still sounds far-fetched to me."

"Why? Think about twins. They can be miles apart and feel what the other is feeling," said Garson. "Don't underestimate the power of love to reach across time and space."

"Over a century apart in time? C'mon, Doc."

"In time and space, there's no past or future, Kip, only the present." Seeing, the cloud of confusion and doubt on the reporter's face, he added: "But that's a subject for another time."

Garson turned his attention back to Riley. "You'll have to work hard at this," he warned. "The constancy and intensity are the difference between success and failure. I know someone who can help you with the technique. He's currently lecturing at MIT. I'll call him tonight."

"How will I know if a connection is made?" asked Riley.

"You'll feel it," replied Garson. "Once you're able to make a strong connection, you should be able to converse with Elizabeth telepathically. That'll be the easy part."

Riley took a deep breath. "What's the hard part?"

"Getting her to accept that you are connecting and conversing with her," replied Garson. "She'll be frightened and confused. She won't understand the physics of this. It might help that belief in the paranormal was popular at that time."

Riley nodded. "I will do whatever I have to do."

"Good." Garson turned to another matter. "We must find the mouth of the wormhole here without delay. Once the CME—the Corona Mass Ejection—is sighted and determined to be Earth-directed, we have anywhere from 24 hours to four days until it arrives." He looked at Kip.

Kip hesitated. "Yeah, yeah, I'm in. But it doesn't mean I believe everything…. How the hell do we find a wormhole opening?"

"Intense energy is emitted as waves of light from inside the rim of the mouth. The area of the mouth will show a big flux in the energy field," explained Garson. "We should be able to detect it with an EMF meter. I borrowed three from the lab at the university."

"Where do we begin?" asked Riley.

Garson pulled out a map. "I've made some calculations and have pinpointed it to be in this area 10 miles west from where you were found."

"It's moving closer to Slaterville," Riley observed. "It's probably being drawn to the charged electromagnetic field there."

"How big an area are we searching?" asked Kip.

"Approximately a radius of 15 miles."

"That's a pretty big area."

"This is why we must start now," said Garson.

"If we find the mouth, what's to keep it from moving again?" quizzed Kip.

Garson looked up at him in all seriousness and replied, "If you're a praying man, pray that it doesn't."

CHAPTER TWENTY

NOW OR NEVER

By two o'clock, Kip, Riley, and Garson were driving the back road toward Slaterville.

"Go another mile," said Garson consulting his map. "We'll start there."

A mile further down the road, Kip pulled off to the side and the three men got out of the car. It was a desolate area. There was a large clearing with thick woods around the perimeter. It looked like a farmer's wheat field that had been cleared for the winter.

Garson laid out the map divided into half-mile sectors on the hood of the car. "I think we should split up."

"Kip, you take the section in this quadrant. Riley, you cover this one. And I'll take the western quadrant. We have approximately three hours of daylight, so let's make the most of it."

Garson armed each of them with an EMF meter, a whistle, and a can of spray paint.

"If you find anything, blow the whistle and mark the spot," he instructed. "Luckily, there aren't any high-tension wires around to make our job more difficult."

Kip and Riley nodded, and the men went their separate ways.

Kip slowly walked his designated quadrant wondering what he was doing there as the needle on his EMF meter continued to register nothing. He heard no whistles sound and guessed that Riley and the professor were having no better luck.

As the sun waned, the air turned colder and the light began to fade. By five o'clock the men were making their way back to the car. Tired and discouraged, no one felt much like talking on the ride back to town.

Kip drove the professor to his hotel.

"Tomorrow morning at eight o'clock?" asked Garson as he got out of the car. "We need to cover some miles."

Kip groaned inwardly. "Yeah, we'll be here," he responded with little enthusiasm.

The next morning, they started again. By noon, no one had any luck, and they broke for lunch at a nearby diner. While they were eating, a text came into Garson's cell phone. His brows drew together in a frown as he read it.

"What is it?" asked Kip.

"A colleague at NOAA says three more solar flares have been detected," replied Garson. "A CME has been associated with one of them, but it's only partially Earth-directed and won't have much impact. We're going to have to pick up the pace, gentlemen."

For the rest of the afternoon, they worked as fast as they could with no more success. At twilight, they called it a day and headed home, just as frustrated as the day before and conscious of the fact that they may be running out of time.

* * * * *

Another day passed without progress. The following day, the dispirited group broke off early to return to Kip's apartment to regroup.

There came a knock on his door, and Kip opened it to find a man of slight stature with Asian features dressed like a monk standing on his doorstep.

"Can I help you?" he asked in surprise.

The monk smiled serenely. "I am here at the behest of Dr. David Garson," he said in fluent English. "I am Dr. Yeshe."

Garson quickly appeared. "Chojie," he greeted with enthusiasm. "Kip, this is Dr. Yeshe Rinpoche. Thank you for coming, Chojie. Come in, come in."

Kip stared in wonder at the Buddhist monk as the man entered the apartment. Hell, he couldn't write a story this crazy, he thought, and Kip considered that when all was said and done, he would need a psychiatrist himself!

"Tashi Delek," said Dr. Yeshe with a respectful bow. "It is good to see you, David. I must confess to being much intrigued, but I do not know how I can help with so little time. The student has no previous Buddhist training. It takes years for one to achieve enlightenment on so high an order."

"I know," acknowledged Garson. "I just need for you to help this person achieve meditation on a level that creates enough vibration in the universe. I wouldn't have bothered such an esteemed one as you, but time is of the essence—and I hoped the scientist in you would be intrigued enough to overlook my presumption."

The Tibetan monk smiled again. "You know me well, my friend. Where is my student?"

Just then Riley entered the room.

"This is your student, Riley Harrington," said Garson. "And he is quite willing."

Dr. Yeshe regarded Riley, taking measure of his depth and determination, and nodded. "I shall require space that is quiet. We cannot be disturbed."

"Not a problem," replied Garson. "Kip and I will be away during the day."

"Then, we shall begin tomorrow morning," declared the monk. "Where might I lay my head, David?"

"I've made reservations for you at a nearby hotel where I'm staying," said Garson.

CHAPTER TWENTY-ONE

A REACH ACROSS TIME

Kip didn't think matters could get any more complicated—then Dr. Porter drove up as he and Dr. Garson were about to get into Kip's car to resume their search for the wormhole.

Kip stifled a groan as she got out of her car and walked up to them.

"Ericka, what are you doing here?" he asked, forcing a smile.

"I came by to check on John," she replied. "Hello, Dr. Garson. I didn't expect to find you here."

"Dr. Porter. It's a pleasure to see you again."

"David and I were just leaving," said Kip.

"So I see. Is John in the apartment?"

Kip and Garson exchanged glances.

"Uh…yes…but he's in the middle of a meditation session," said Kip.

She looked at him quizzically. "A meditation session?"

"Uh, yeah, David thought it might help John to relax more and make it easier for him to remember things about his life," explained Kip. "Why don't you come back later?"

Ericka eyed the two men with suspicion. "Okay, what's going on? Is John all right? He *is* still here, isn't he?"

Kip and Garson exchanged glances again.

"Dr. Porter, might I assume that you consider yourself to be a serious student of science?" asked Dr. Garson.

"Of course. I am a psychiatrist," she replied somewhat indignant.

"How good is your physics?"

"I was a physics major before switching to medicine and psychology. Why is that pertinent?" she demanded to know.

"She's not quantum, Doc," warned Kip, reading the professor's mind.

"We could use the extra help, Kip."

"It's up to you, Doc, but I wouldn't if I were you. She's a tough nut to crack."

Ericka let out a huff of annoyance. "Hello, I'm standing right here. What's up with you two? You might as well say. I'm not leaving until I get the truth."

"Be careful what you wish for," advised Kip.

"Why don't we drive over to that coffee house in town?" suggested Garson. "We can talk over a cup of coffee."

Ericka regarded them warily for a moment. "Okay, let's go."

With coffee and a plate of pastries in front of them, Ericka turned a stern eye on Kip and Garson. "Start talking, guys."

"John can't remember his life here because he *is* Riley Harrington. He accidentally fell into the mouth of a wormhole in 1903 that had opened during a solar storm and ended up here because the storm we had last month was occurring at the same time and opened the mouth at this end," Kip blurted out.

Ericka stared wide-eyed at him and huffed with exasperation. "Stop toying with me, Kip. I'm not in the mood."

Kip looked over at Garson. "That's your cue, Doc."

Dr. Garson gave him a look of reproof.

"She wanted the unvarnished truth," said Kip, unapologetic.

"Guys! What is going on?" demanded Ericka.

Dr. Garson cleared his throat. "Permit me to explain everything with a little more context…from the viewpoint of a scientist, Dr. Porter."

He took out a pad and pencil. Using mathematical equations and diagrams, he explained the science of wormholes and closed time-like curves and how solar storms could trigger the opening of portals.

Ericka put up a hand. "Stop. I hope you're not saying what I think you're saying, Dr. Garson."

"I'm afraid that I am, Dr. Porter. As Kip said, John is Riley. The sunspot cycle in 1903 mirrors our sunspot cycle of today. The geomagnetic storm that occurred in 1903 occurred here a few weeks ago. That's how Riley came to be here. Hopefully, he can return to his time when concurring storms occur again to reopen the portals."

Ericka looked at Kip in astonishment. "Don't tell me that you, of all people, are buying into this?"

Kip shrugged and ticked off his findings. "The Slaterville Police Department still has the evidence box from the Harrington shooting in 1903. I checked it. Riley's coat is in there as well as the gun that he was shot with. The coat shows a bullet hole in the same place where John was shot. And a piece of cloth taken from Riley's coat matches the material on the pants that John was wearing when I found him."

Ericka was dumbfounded. "No…no, there has to be another explanation."

"A ballistics test on the gun proved that the bullet removed from John came from that gun, which, according to an expert, hasn't been fired in a lot of years," continued Kip. "You explain it."

Ericka looked from Kip to the professor too astounded to speak for a moment. "Are you telling me I could have fallen into a freaking time tunnel that day in the grove?"

Garson smiled. "You were in no danger, Dr. Porter. The mouths of the worm holes are closed for the time being. But NOAA says a storm is imminent on our end."

"We just have one little problem," interjected Kip. "The mouth of the wormhole here has moved. We've been searching for it for days. That's where we were going when you drove up."

Ericka put a hand to her forehead trying to sort her thoughts. "So, you and Dr. Garson were going out to look for the mouth of a wormhole that has moved."

She let out a short laugh. "Okay, I'll play along. How were you expecting to find this…this wormhole?"

"With EMF meters," replied Garson.

"So you find this mouth, a solar storm occurs, and Riley magically reappears in 1903," she reiterated airily.

"Well, not exactly," said Kip. "There's this thing called the space-time continuum."

Garson could see her exasperation building and stepped in to explain again.

"Dr. Porter, what Kip is trying to say is that because Riley came from a different dimension of time, a year or years may have passed while he's been here. We don't know the date to which he'll return, and the farther Riley returns from the date he disappeared, the greater the danger it will create a ripple effect that will change history. So, it's imperative that he returns with this next storm."

Ericka's mouth dropped open. She closed her eyes and took a deep breath, holding on to her composure by a thread.

"Let me get this straight," she said. "There's a solar storm coming—you don't know when—that will activate a portal—you don't know where—that will send Riley back to a time you can't predict."

"Actually, Dr. Porter, there was a significant solar event recorded in 1907 Slaterville that seems likely to correspond with the one we are expecting here. We think that might be the date," responded Garson.

"But you can't say that for sure."

"No, not yet," he admitted.

"Not yet! How can you possibly hope to determine it?" Ericka demanded to know, her voice rising with her agitation.

Garson hesitated. "If we can make contact, Elizabeth Slater will tell us."

Ericka stared at him. She had no idea what to say to that. Dr. Garson wasn't some crackpot she could easily dismiss as a flake. He was a highly acclaimed physicist well published in the field of quantum mechanics.

She let out a humorless laugh. "I can't believe I'm even asking this, but how can you contact a woman in another dimension of time, Doctor?"

Garson calmly explained about quantum entanglement and the use of meditation. He wrote out a website on a napkin and pushed it across the table to her. "You can read the study for yourself."

Ericka glanced at the website and shook her head. "No...no, I can't allow you to do this. It could do irreparable harm to John."

"Forgive me, Dr. Porter, but he is more rooted in reality than you are at the moment," said Garson. "However much you try to deny it, John is Riley. And Dr. Yeshe is an excellent and highly esteemed teacher in the art of meditation."

Ericka's eyes widened. "Dr. Yeshe? He's a part of this?"

"Yes. You know him?"

"I attended his seminar at the University of Pennsylvania a few years ago. I can't believe he has agreed to take part in this."

"Buddhism is a bridge to quantum physics, Dr. Porter. Despite what some people want to believe, spirituality and science go hand in hand."

Kip smiled. "It kind of hits you in the gut, doesn't it? Give it up, Ericka. You can't go up against quantum physics and win."

She glared at him.

"Believe me, Dr. Porter, I can appreciate how crazy this all sounds—"

"No, you can't, Dr. Garson. This is beyond crazy. This is insanity. I have committed people for observation who are less delusional than this."

"It is fact firmly rooted in scientific principles, Dr. Porter. Even Einstein recognized that time travel is possible."

"Principles aside, science is not always grounded in reality," she retorted.

"What is reality?" asked Garson. "As a psychiatrist, you know everyone has a different perception of it. The failing of humans is that they tend to place a boundary around their perceived world as to what they are willing to accept as real. The ones who don't limit themselves are called pioneers and visionaries. Where would we be today without them?"

"I'm not going to debate philosophy with you, Dr. Garson. What you are telling me is only theoretically possible."

"Not anymore. Riley is proof of it," replied Garson.

Ericka didn't know what Riley was proof of. She looked at Kip and the professor—both men respected in their fields, both thought to be of sound mind and practice. Add to them Dr. Yeshe who was much renowned in academic circles.

She reached for her coat. "I'm coming with you to search for this wormhole opening, if only to hear you admit that you've had a lapse in…in judgment. And that's being kind."

Meanwhile

Dr. Yeshe explained the general concept of meditation to Riley.

"Since we don't know how much time we have, we must concentrate on focusing your mind," he said. "A disciplined mind is very powerful. A distracted mind is powerless to do anything.

"To achieve this level of calming, position is important," the monk continued to explain. "If your torso is straight, it allows for a free flow of energy and helps to balance the mind. You may choose to sit on the floor in the traditional cross-legged position or lie on the couch."

"I prefer the couch," said Riley.

The monk nodded. "Lie down in a straight line."

Riley took off his shoes and lay down.

"Slowly, consciously inhale and exhale," instructed Yeshe.

He pressed a yellow Post-it Note to the wall at the end of couch at Riley's eye level.

"Stare at this while you concentrate on your breathing," he said. "Resist any effort for your mind to scatter. Imagine a barrier keeping out distracting thoughts. Let nothing else enter your mind."

After several minutes, Yeshe continued. "Now visualize Elizabeth. Feel her presence, the warmth of her smile, the touch of her hand. Smell the fragrance of her perfume."

Riley smiled as Elizabeth appeared in his mind's eye, and his heart swelled with longing so intense it brought tears to his eyes. Then, the image faded away, and a black void enveloped him.

He sat up distraught. "I couldn't hold the image. I couldn't hold it. What does it mean?"

"Not to worry, Mr. Harrington. You are new to meditation. It will take some practice," said Yeshe. "To retain visualization on a special object requires stability and clarity. Your mind must be balanced. It can't be too loose or too tight."

"I don't know what that means," retorted Riley.

Dr. Yeshe paused, searching for a point of comparison.

"You are a physicist, Mr. Harrington. You are accustomed to the practice of what we call intense mindfulness. Focusing on a theorem or equation is no different than focusing on a special object in meditation. You can apply the same principles."

The analogy was something Riley understood, and he felt more encouraged.

"Relax for now," counseled Dr. Yeshe. "We'll try again in an hour. Have you a picture of Elizabeth?"

Riley nodded. "Kip made a copy of her portrait that hangs in the Slater house."

"Perhaps it might help you to look at the picture before beginning a session."

* * * * *

The next day went much the same. Garson and his team had not found the wormhole, and Riley had not connected with Elizabeth. Ericka wasn't surprised. She hadn't expected success in either case but decided to let it all playout—in the interest of science.

Everyone sat disheartened in Kip's living room that evening.

"What is the use to keep trying? I don't believe Elizabeth is there anymore," said Riley. "Whatever befell her in 1907, I fear has already come to pass."

"We don't know that," said Dr. Garson. "We can't stop now. Regardless, we need to pinpoint the time to which you will return."

Riley rose from his seat in agitation. "I'm not going back if I can't be with Elizabeth. I don't care about your ripple effect."

Garson and Dr. Yeshi exchanged glances. Riley had to go back, but if he refused how were they to force him?

"Perhaps I can do more to help Riley make the initial contact, if there is one to be made," said Dr. Yeshe. "I can enter into meditation along with Riley to add more vibration to the waves. If Elizabeth is there, I will feel her." He looked at Riley. "Maybe knowing she is there will serve to encourage you."

Riley nodded, more heartened. "When can we start?"

"Now, if the others will oblige us."

Kip stood up. "Anyone care to join me for a drink at the Fairfield Brewery? I'm buying."

"Count me in," said Garson.

"I could use a mood adjustment," responded Ericka.

When they left the apartment, Dr. Yeshe and Riley went to work with renewed determination. This time Riley sat cross-legged on floor next to Dr. Yeshe.

After about a half hour, Dr. Yeshe touched Riley's arm. "Do you feel her?"

Riley smiled. "Yes," he said, filled with wonder and joy. "I can feel Elizabeth's presence."

"Good. Continue to hold her vibration," instructed Dr. Yeshe. "I'm going to disengage now to allow your power to grow."

CHAPTER TWENTY-TWO

GOING BACK TO THE PAST

Slaterville—1907

Thomas Marshall laid down his newspaper and looked at his wife in disbelief at the latest of her outrageous requests.

"What did you say?"

"I want to get a job," she repeated.

He would have burst out laughing but for the determined look on her face.

"What are you trying to do to me, Elizabeth…drive me crazy? First, you wanted to go to Philadelphia to attend a rally of radical women agitating for the right to vote. I had to threaten to lock you in your room. Then, you tried to form your own group of suffragettes, and I had to step in to put a stop to that. Now, you want to take a job like a member of the underclass?"

"Thomas, I don't see the harm in—"

He pounded his fist on the table. "For God's sake, Elizabeth, our fathers were founders of this town. I'm president of the largest bank in Slaterville and sit on the board of several businesses. We are leading citizens. We have wealth and position. I'll not allow you and your harebrained ideas to jeopardize that."

Elizabeth Slater Marshall shoved aside her plate, not in the mood for breakfast this morning. "I have nothing of substance to do with my time, Thomas. I want to contribute something important...maybe go back to school. I just read that more and more women are being admitted to law schools."

Her husband gave a derisive snort. "You have enough education. If you don't stop this nonsense, I shall be forced to monitor what you read."

"Thomas—"

"Go shopping, Elizabeth. It'll make you feel better. If you want to contribute something, contribute to the economy of the town."

Thomas picked up his newspaper, putting an end to the conversation. It was the way such discussions always went.

Elizabeth glanced around the well-appointed dining room, designed to showcase the owner's wealth, as was the rest of the house. Thomas was right. She had money, position—everything a woman could want—except the power to control her life. Without that, the rest was meaningless to her.

The maid came in to clear away the dishes. Thomas set aside his paper and stood up to leave.

"Don't forget about dinner tonight with the Franklins. Their guests are Charles Morse—an important financier from New York—and his wife, so let's not have one of your headaches," he warned. "And, Elizabeth, don't offer your views on anything other than the weather."

As he left the room, Elizabeth glared at him. When she heard the front door close on him, she rose from the table and went to her bedroom.

It was a large, bright room when the sun was out. Today, everything was dreary, seeming to channel her mood. Not even the fire in the fireplace could banish the gloom.

Elizabeth went to her vanity. From a secret compartment, she took out a picture. The face of a young man stared back at her. He was a handsome man with a closely trimmed mustache and goatee, and she traced the contours of his features with her finger. Her mind's eye could see the twinkle in his eyes and the smile on his lips, and her heart constricted. Tears spilled down her cheeks.

How differently her life might be now had she been able to meet him that night. The thought tortured her daily. It had sustained her to believe that Riley was alive and would come back for her, but after all this time with no word from him, that slender strand of hope was fraying. She put her head in her hands and sobbed.

There came a quiet knock on the door, and the maid opened it.

"Madam, you have a guest—"

Without waiting to be formally announced, a vivacious redhead swept into the room.

"Honestly, darling, who else would be calling? Thomas practically holds you prisoner," said Julia Trowbridge. "It's a wonder he still allows me to visit."

Elizabeth brightened and quickly wiped away tears. "Willa, you may go."

The maid bobbed. "Yes, ma'am."

Elizabeth turned to her dearest friend. "Thomas allows you to visit because he wants to keep track of what your husband is doing. He fancies Lawrence to be his greatest competitor."

Julia looked at her in surprise. "In what?"

"Making money, of course," replied Elizabeth, in a derisive tone. "What else matters to such men? But tell me. What brings you here this morning?"

"A sale at Barnsworth's," replied Julia. "You have been looking pale and hollow-eyed lately. You need to get out. And don't worry about Thomas. He's in Harrisburg for the day. I checked. So, you don't need a permission slip."

"Actually, Thomas told me to go shopping," said Elizabeth.

Julia raised a brow. "Are you certain you heard him correctly?"

Elizabeth nodded. "His exact words were: 'If you want to do something, go shopping and help the economy of the town.'"

Julia snorted. "That doesn't sound like Thomas. He must have been preoccupied with another matter."

"I told him I wanted to either get a job or go to law school."

Julia looked at her in mock horror. "No! You silly, silly girl. Imagine that a woman of your position should want to exercise her mind and make a contribution to the world."

Her brown eyes twinkled with amusement. "Oh, how I would like to have been a fly on the wall during that conversation. Thomas must have had a conniption."

Elizabeth giggled. "Yes, quite so. I suppose he figured shopping would be the lesser of two evils to clear my head of such silly notions."

"Well, then, it is my opinion that it shall take many purchases to accomplish that task," pronounced Julia.

Elizabeth regarded her friend with affection. "Dear, dear Julia, what would I do without you? My days would be that much bleaker."

Julia's heart wrenched at the look of despair in her friend's eyes. "You still think about him, don't you?"

Elizabeth nodded and blinked back tears. "I try not to. But lately, he comes to mind with little urging."

"I know Thomas isn't a great alternative, but you can't stay stuck in the past, Elizabeth. You don't even know if Riley is alive. That drifter did confess to shooting him."

"He swore he didn't kill him, Julia."

"Of course he would say that to escape the noose."

"But Riley's remains were never found," argued Elizabeth.

Julia sighed. "Honey, there have been no reported sightings of him in four years. The detective I hired on your behalf found no sign of him. If Riley was alive, don't you think he would have found a way to contact you?"

"I didn't meet him that night as I promised I would, Julia. He may think that I betrayed him."

Julia frowned. This was one of her friend's darker days.

"You need to find something else to fill your life," she said. "Today, I vote for shopping. Tomorrow, we'll find some other way to torture Thomas."

Elizabeth forced a smile. "You are right. Yes, let us to it then. I shall ring for Willa to bring my hat and coat…"

Her voice trailed off as a buzzing sound suddenly filled her head and lights rushed toward her at a high rate of speed. Near to fainting, she grabbed onto the back of a chair and closed her eyes.

"Elizabeth, what befalls you?" asked Julia anxiously. "Elizabeth!"

Her friend's voice seemed to come from far away. Then the sensation passed almost as quickly as it came on.

"I'm fine," said Elizabeth.

"No, you're not," retorted Julia, her face a mask of concern. "You're as white as a sheet, and you're shaking." She took Elizabeth's arm and helped her to sit down in the chair. "Shall I fetch the maid?"

Elizabeth shook her head. "I-I've been having these strange attacks for the past couple of days. They come without notice or provocation."

"Then you should see a doctor," insisted Julia.

"No, it would only serve to annoy Thomas. He thinks illness to be a state of mind."

Julia hesitated. "Forgive me, but is it possible that you are with child?"

Elizabeth's mouth twisted into a wry smile. "No, Julia, it is not that…. Come, if we are to go shopping, we must leave. Thomas has commanded my appearance at the Franklins for dinner tonight."

Julia groaned. "Ugh, you poor dear. The Franklins are boring snobs seeking to run with the big dogs." She paused with a thought. "Thomas fits right in, doesn't he?"

Elizabeth laughed. "Birds of a feather. The Franklins' guests are a financier and his wife from New York. 'There is an opportunity to be had here,'" she said, mimicking her husband.

"You are sure you are feeling well to shop?" asked Julia. "Perhaps you should rest the day."

Elizabeth shook her head. "An outing with my friend will do me better."

"Still," said Julia on a serious note, "I shall summon a doctor for you myself if these attacks persist."

CHAPTER TWENTY-THREE

VOICES

Elizabeth stifled a yawn as she looked around the Franklins' dining room, bored out of her mind, praying that the evening would soon end.

Throughout dinner, she had struggled to follow the stilted, mundane conversation. Thomas had sent her looks of warning the few times a question was directed to her and nodded in approval when she answered to his satisfaction.

Finally, Mrs. Franklin suggested that the ladies retire to the parlor and leave the men to their cigars and talk of business. Servants pulled back their chairs, and Elizabeth and Mrs. Morse rose to follow Mrs. Franklin from the dining room.

At the doorway, Elizabeth was hit with another one of her strange attacks. She gripped the doorframe and closed her eyes to shut out the dizzying spiraling light. This one wanted to hang on a few seconds longer.

When she could open her eyes, she glanced around her, relieved to find that no one had taken notice. The men were too engaged in their conversation, and Mrs. Franklin and Mrs. Morse had continued on into the parlor.

When Elizabeth entered the room, Mrs. Franklin looked at her quizzically. "I thought you were behind us, Mrs. Marshall."

"I stopped to admire the vase in the foyer," said Elizabeth. "I hope you don't find it presumptuous of me."

Mrs. Franklin beamed with delight. "Certainly not. I purchased it in England while on a European tour. I am pleased you find it to your liking, Mrs. Marshall. Tea?"

Elizabeth nodded. "Yes, thank you."

It was nearly eleven o'clock when the Marshalls returned home. Elizabeth was tired from the long, tedious evening. She was in no mood to have her behavior critiqued, as was the usual practice, and was relieved to find that her husband was too distracted to bother with it this night.

"Charles Morse and the Heinze brothers have a plan to corner United Copper and make a killing on it in the stock market, and they are looking for venture capitalists," he told her.

His eyes glowed as he savored the possibilities.

"This could be just the beginning for me, Elizabeth. These are big time financiers. They sit on the boards of the biggest banks in New York. They don't invite just anyone to invest."

"Indeed," she murmured, uninterested.

"I would advise you to invest your inheritance as well, Elizabeth. This venture could be worth millions. Morse shorted his ice company and walked away with $12 million two years ago."

"Thomas, I am very tired. If I may retire—"

"Yes, yes, go to your room," he said, dismissing her with the wave of his hand. "I have much to think on."

As he hurried off to his study, Elizabeth climbed the stairs to her bedroom.

The maid helped her prepare for bed. When Elizabeth slipped beneath the covers, she soon fell into a deep sleep. Two hours later, the call of her name, so sharp and clear, startled her awake.

She sat up, her heart thudding hard against her chest. "Who is there?" she asked in a trembling voice. "Who calls to me?"

No one answered. She quickly turned on a light and looked around the room. No one was there. It had seemed so real, the voice so distinct it was a long time until she could fall back to sleep.

The next morning, Elizabeth arose gratified to find that Thomas had already left for the bank. She couldn't get last night's dream, for lack of a better word for it, out of her mind and wasn't up to facing her husband and his demands.

She sat at her vanity slowly brushing out her hair, deep in thought, when she was startled again by a voice asking, "Can you hear me?"

She turned sharply to the maid who was straightening the bed. "Did you say something, Clara?"

"No, ma'am."

"I thought I heard someone speaking just now," said Elizabeth.

"I didna hear nothin', ma'am. I've finished with the room. Shall I help you to dress now?"

Elizabeth shook her head. "Not yet. Perhaps in an hour. Please have a breakfast tray sent up."

"Yes, ma'am."

Elizabeth sat at the vanity for a long time, trying to make sense of the strange occurrences. Perhaps Julia was right. Maybe she did need to see a doctor. But what would she tell him—that she was experiencing odd things and heard someone talk to her when no one was there? No, he would think her crazy, and it would hand Thomas another cudgel to keep her in line.

Over the next few days, the episodes increased. Elizabeth became more and more withdrawn. Even Thomas began to notice.

"You haven't been yourself lately," he said to her one morning at breakfast. "If you are coming down with something, perhaps you should stay abed until you are feeling better. I have to go to New York tomorrow to finalize my deal with Charles Morse. I don't want to catch something from you and become too indisposed to make the trip."

"Yes, Thomas, perhaps you are right. I wouldn't want to indispose you," she responded with a touch of sarcasm. She laid her napkin aside and stood up. "Please excuse me."

Thomas nodded and picked up the newspaper. "Don't say anything about my business arrangement to your friend Julia," he instructed. "Trowbridge would love to have a piece of this, and I'm not inclined to allow it."

"As you wish, Thomas."

Elizabeth quickly left the room.

She crossed the foyer and climbed the staircase, pausing on the landing to gaze wistfully out the window. It was Sunday. Couples strolled through the park-like square across the street, and children gamboled about playing games and rolling hoops. She felt a stab of pain in her heart at the thought of the very different life she might have had.

Elizabeth suddenly heard a loud buzzing in her head and hurried to her room. She dropped into a chair and put her hands to her ears to block out the sound. What was wrong with her?

"Stop!" she cried out. "Please, dear God, stop tormenting me!"

CHAPTER TWENTY-FOUR

FEAR AND CONFUSION

Riley quickly pulled out of his state of meditation, instead of slowly disengaging as instructed.

"Is something wrong?" asked Dr Yeshe.

"I sense great fear in Elizabeth when I speak to her. I cannot continue to frighten her."

"It is unavoidable until she embraces certain truths," said Dr. Yeshe.

Riley raked a hand through his hair. "How can I help her to do that when she is too fearful to engage?" he fretted.

"Continue to meditate," Dr. Yeshe instructed. "Keep Elizabeth in your thoughts to maintain the connection. Surround her image with love, but don't speak to her. I am returning to my hotel. We shall continue our sessions in a few days."

That evening, the Tibetan monk elevated himself to the highest level of consciousness, bringing great vibration to the advanced wavelength that connected to Elizabeth. He could feel her distress when he awoke her with the call of her name, and he surrounded her with a veil of warmth and love.

As he felt her begin to be comforted by it, he communicated with her telepathically. He told her there was nothing for her to fear, that she was not mentally ill, but experiencing a special connection with

God and the universe. She didn't answer, but he knew she heard him; he felt her level of anxiety rise.

After a long moment, she hesitantly asked: "Who are you? Are you...God?"

"No. I am a guide," he answered.

"An angel?"

"No. I am a being who has come to guide you to enlightenment and happiness, if you will allow me," replied the monk.

Elizabeth let out a strangled cry. "Am I dying?"

"No, no, quite the contrary," Dr. Yeshe assured her.

A sob caught in her throat. "Please, I don't understand. What is happening to me?"

The monk could feel her heart beating hard.

"You will understand soon, but you must try to stay calm," he said. "The voice of another will come to you. Do not be afraid. Neither he nor I will ever lie to you or deceive you. We will tell you only truths. You must trust us."

Elizabeth gasped. "That is what the devil says."

"You will know the difference," Dr. Yeshe reassured her. "When we come to you, you will feel safe. You will feel love. You will never feel darkness, fear, or hatred. We will never ask you to do anything you think is wrong or evil."

"Why do I hear you?" she cried. "Only the mentally ill hear voices in their heads."

"I promise you are not ill, my child. You can hear us for reasons beyond your comprehension at the moment. This is why you must trust us."

"To what end?" she questioned with apprehension.

"To the life you desire," replied the monk.

Tears rolled down Elizabeth's cheeks. "You must be demonic to mock me so heartlessly."

"I am naught but a messenger, Elizabeth, here to lead you from your darkness into love, light, and happiness if you so permit. I will leave you now. Remember my words but tell no one of this. People will not understand."

Elizabeth was too terrified and confused to sleep. She wavered between the world of spirituality and the world of reality, weighing sometimes more on the side of the latter with a niggling fear that she was, in fact, mentally ill.

The "being" had told her that she wasn't ill and that he had come to lead her to a place of happiness, but she could know happiness only with Riley. How was that possible? Was the voice she had heard her own telling her what she wanted to hear?

She was profoundly unhappy in her life, and, according to a European doctor who had come into prominence—Sigmund Freud—that made her more vulnerable to delusions. How had Freud put it…people in mental anguish sought refuge in fantasy. Was this what she was doing?

In the wee hours of the morning, she finally fell into a fitful sleep.

All too soon, sunlight flooded the room when the maid pulled open the drapes. "Madam, you must make haste.

Elizabeth moaned. "For what?"

"You are attending a luncheon. Miss Julia will be here soon."

She barely got the words out before Julia strode into the room. "Elizabeth, you aren't ready!"

"I had a fitful night, Julia. Please go on without me."

Julia put her hands on her hips. "Not on your life. You have begged off too many invites. People will begin to think you're antisocial…. Come, it should be fun. It's a progressive group. And Violet is employing a psychic to entertain us. So up with you."

Elizabeth sighed. She didn't have the energy to argue.

Throughout the luncheon, the conversation was lively and substantive, running the gamut from politics to women's rights instead of being limited to gossip and fashion. And Elizabeth was glad now that Julia had forced her to attend. The discussion ended with the topic of spirituality, a perfect segue into the host's planned entertainment.

When the two dozen guests were ushered from the dining room into the parlor, they found chairs arranged in a large circle. Once everyone was seated, the host brought in and introduced the psychic.

The woman was middle-aged, wore wire-rim glasses, and had a pleasing countenance. Unlike the more flamboyant members of her trade, she was plainly dressed in a gray skirt and white blouse and possessed a self-effacing manner that evoked more the image of a church lady than a medium. Elizabeth couldn't decide if this made her more credible or less so than her counterparts.

A few of the ladies giggled nervously as the psychic slowly walked inside the circle from guest to guest touching each on the shoulder— another deviation from the usual use of Tarot cards and crystal balls.

She told one woman where to find a necklace that had been misplaced. She gave another lady a message from the lady's mother who had recently passed. For another guest, she diagnosed a health concern that was perplexing her doctors. Despite the ladies' exclamations of amazement, Elizabeth remained skeptical.

When the psychic came to her, the medium fell silent for a few moments. "There is someone—a man— trying to contact you."

"If it is my father, I do not wish to hear from him," responded Elizabeth with a hard edge to her tone.

The psychic shook her head, her brow puckering in bewilderment. "No, it is not someone who has passed over. This person is…. this person is reaching out to you from another dimension of time." She looked at Elizabeth. "Do you understand this?"

"No," said Elizabeth.

The psychic continued to regard her, puzzled and curious. "Neither do I. I have never experienced this before." She hesitated a moment longer, then moved on to the next lady.

Julia nudged her friend. "What was that all about?"

Elizabeth shrugged. "I have no idea."

Over the course of the remaining guests' readings, the psychic paused now and then to give Elizabeth quizzical looks.

When the readings drew to a close, the psychic took Julia aside. "Mrs. Trowbridge, I sense you have a close friendship with Mrs. Marshall."

"Yes, quite close," replied Julia.

"It is important that you stay by her side," warned the psychic. "Mrs. Marshall is going to need your help. There is the presence of a force I do not clearly understand. It appears nonthreatening, but yet I sense great danger around her."

The medium was so serious and concerned a chill ran through Julia. She instantly recalled the strange episodes her friend had experienced. Despite Elizabeth's assurances that she was fine, Julia was acutely aware that Elizabeth was not herself of late.

CHAPTER TWENTY-FIVE

AN UNSEEN GUIDE

Dr. Yeshe continued to try to prepare Elizabeth, telepathically breaking into her thoughts when he thought she might be alone and more relaxed, trying to make her more comfortable with the thought of an unseen guide and an alternative reality.

At first, she would be uncommunicative, fearful that she was hastening her fall into madness by responding. When Dr. Yeshe assured her that this was not the case, she would become angry that she was being forced to experience this uncommon phenomenon of which she had no understanding or control over.

After a few days of silence, curiosity would push her to engage again. When her questions were met with ambiguous answers, and her demands for tangible proof that this was real were met with the continued response that she would have to trust that it was, she would angrily withdraw again, refusing to communicate until a need to understand drove her forward once more. And, thus, went this cycle for a number of days.

Finally, Elizabeth became more resigned to it. She was less fearful that the voice was an evil entity. It never asked her to consider or do anything she felt was wrong as it had promised her. To the contrary, it counseled her against allowing negative emotions to overcome positive ones. Still, she feared being lulled into a false sense of security and remained wary, refusing to totally surrender her trust.

Then the voice stopped. It hadn't visited her in three days, and Elizabeth found herself at odds with her feelings. While she welcomed the normalcy, she felt a distinct void in its absence.

When the entity finally spoke to her this night, she was of a mood to listen. It warned her of a coming event that would require her to consider a reality far different than the one she knew. Her apprehension mounted when she was told that she would have to set aside every truth she had been taught and open her mind to the unimaginable.

Elizabeth telepathically pelted the voice with questions, but to each came the response: "All will be told to you when the time is right…when you are prepared to hear the truth."

Frustrated, her mood turned to anger again. "I will have the truth now, or I shall not continue to listen," she threatened.

"People think they want the truth until it is told to them," the entity replied. "You are not yet prepared for it."

"What truth can be so difficult to accept?" she demanded to know.

"The truth that your world is just one of many and your reality but an illusion."

Elizabeth had no idea what to make of such a statement. She demanded an explanation, but the voice was silent. Rather than feeling enlightened, she felt much more uncertain.

CHAPTER TWENTY-SIX

IS THIS MADNESS?

The team sat around Kip's kitchen table, waiting for Dr. Garson to finish his call. When he hung up, they knew it wasn't good news.

"What is it?" asked Dr. Yeshe.

"That was my friend at NOAA. Solar flare activity has intensified. We are lucky that no coronal mass ejections have materialized, but I don't know how long our luck can hold," reported Garson.

He rubbed his forehead as he considered the situation. "My instincts tell me we don't have much time."

"In more ways than one," said Kip. "The weather is turning."

Garson frowned. "Chojie, you and Riley need to move faster on your preparation of Elizabeth. We need to know what's happening on that end. The rest of us will continue our search for the wormhole."

Armed with maps and EMF meters, Dr. Porter, Kip, and Garson headed out to the car once more.

Dr. Yeshe looked at Riley. "I have laid enough of a foundation. I think it is time for you to contact Elizabeth now."

"Are you certain that she is ready? You said she was still distrustful."

"I believe she will be more trusting if she knows it is you. You have to remember that you will be just a voice in her head, but she will know it is you by the inflections in your tone and by the words and phrases that she associates with you. If there is a special name you called her or a turn of words, use them."

Riley hesitated. "What if…what if, after we convince Elizabeth to accept all of this, Dr. Garson can't find the opening of the wormhole in time?"

Dr. Yeshe put his hand on Riley's shoulder. "Part of the battle is keeping faith that he will. Are you ready?"

Riley nodded and allowed Dr. Yeshe to lead him into deep meditation.

Elizabeth awoke from another fitful sleep, feeling anxious and restless. Her heart beat rapidly, and she felt that strange feeling travel through her body. The entity had explained that it was her vibration connecting with his. She threw aside the covers and jumped out of bed.

"Don't be afraid," she heard the voice in her head say.

It seemed different this time—more intimate.

"Liza, do you hear me?"

Elizabeth stiffened, and she felt so paralyzed with fear that she thought her heart would stop. Only one person had ever called her by that name. She let out a cry and fled back to her bed.

"Do not be fearful. I mean you no harm, Liza."

She gasped and clutched the covers to her. "This is the work of the devil," she responded telepathically. "Why do you torment me so?"

"I am not the devil, my love. I promise you," replied the voice.

"Then most assuredly I am cursed with a disease of the mind."

"I promise you that is not the case either," the entity assured her.

"Who are you?"

"You know who I am, Liza."

"No! You cannot be. Riley is dead. Oh, dear God, what madness is this?"

"Liza, listen to me. I was shot, yes, but I did not die. I went somewhere else."

"I don't believe you. I don't believe you are Riley," Elizabeth sobbed, terrified. "Why do you torture me?"

Riley struggled to remain calm as he frantically sought a way to both soothe and convince her. Recalling Dr. Yeshe's instructions, he took a different tact and began reciting incidences of their more intimate moments known only to them.

Elizabeth gasped. "How is this possible? How is any of this possible?"

"Remember what the guide told you, Liza. You must suspend your beliefs," said Riley. "Believe me when I tell you that this is possible and that soon I am coming to be with you. I will be the proof you seek."

"I don't understand," she cried.

"In time, you will. Until then, you must trust me and do as I tell you to do." He felt her recoil and hurried to reassure her. "I will never ask you to do anything that will place you in harm's way. I will never ask you to do anything that you feel is wrong."

The voice was loving. It sounded like Riley, the way he talked, the phrases he used. She clutched the blankets to her wanting desperately to believe and sobbed harder.

Riley couldn't hold her or stroke her hair, and he worked hard to comfort her telepathically with his voice inflections and words. Finally, she had calmed enough that he could converse with her in a more productive manner.

"Liza, what is the date there?"

She thought it an odd question, totally out of keeping with the tenor of her other conversations with either voice. "It is November 15th," she replied haltingly.

"1907?" Riley asked hopefully.

"Yes. Why do you ask?" she questioned warily. "Shouldn't you already know that?"

Riley debated how much to tell her. She still was a long way from being able to understand. "Elizabeth, listen to me. I am in a time different from you. I don't expect you to understand that, but the month, the day, and the year are not the same."

Elizabeth drew in her breath sharply. The psychic had told her that the person who was trying to contact her was in another dimension of time.

"The other voice spoke to you of an event that is coming," continued Riley. "This event will enable me to travel from my dimension to yours so that we can be reunited. To determine when this will occur requires that I know what is happening in your dimension of time. For this, I must depend upon reports from you."

Riley paused to give her a moment to absorb everything.

"What kind of event is coming?" she asked hesitantly.

"Do you remember in November of 1903 when the telegraph stopped working and there was a strange, electrical feeling in the air and this rainbow of lights lit up the sky?"

"Yes."

"That was because of a naturally occurring phenomenon called a solar storm, and it opened a kind of portal," he said. He knew she would never comprehend such a thing as a wormhole.

"I know this sounds crazy, Liza, but it is the truth," he continued. "When I was shot, I fell into a vortex of energy that transported me to where I am now. There is another such storm soon to occur there that shall allow me to transport back. You must tell me when you notice disturbances similar to those that occurred in 1903."

Elizabeth didn't know how to react to that. She had read *The Time Machine* by H.G. Wells, but that was fiction. She couldn't imagine traveling from one time to another in real life. But what did the other voice tell her: reality is an illusion? What did that even mean?

Elizabeth couldn't begin to contemplate what questions to ask and so remained silent. Riley sensed she needed space to gather her thoughts. With a promise to come again soon, he told her he loved her and withdrew from the connection.

The next two days went much the same when Riley reconnected with her. She said little. She mostly listened. By the third night, she was more engaged, and Riley patiently answered her questions as well as she might understand.

The sound of his voice wrapped her in a cloak of such solace and love she no longer cared that she might be crazy. This was her private refuge, real or not, and she took strength from it. And as incredible as it might sound, she clung to his promise like a life preserver that he would come for her.

CHAPTER TWENTY-SEVEN

LEVERAGE

As Thomas Marshall read the latest news to come across the ticker tape machine, his face turned more ashen in color.

The scheme to corner the market on copper had backfired spectacularly, creating a panic on Wall Street.

Charles Morse and Augustus Heinze had been forced to resign from their various bank directorships. Depositors had raced to withdraw their funds from the banks of the New York investors.

A few weeks later, the run on other New York Trusts had begun, and every day brought news of more and more bank failures. Within a month, 13 had failed. Brokerage houses were closing at an astonishing rate. The stock market had nearly collapsed twice.

J. P. Morgan had tried to backstop the panic, and for a short time, his efforts were successful. But now all appeared lost. The gold supply was at a new low; money was getting scarce. The U.S. Treasury had depleted most of its working capital to stem the panic and could offer no more help.

Marshall dropped the ticker tape and anxiously paced the floor of his office at the bank. He was ruined. He had put in every penny he had and had dipped into his own bank's limited cash reserves when Charles Morse had pressured him for more funds to shore up copper prices.

Contagion was beginning to spread. People across the country were withdrawing their money in record numbers. If there was a run on his bank, his embezzlement would be exposed.

Marshall collapsed heavily into a chair. Sweat broke out on his forehead, and he anxiously rifled a hand through his hair as he imagined a picture of himself being led off to jail on the front page of the newspaper. The financial ruination and the loss of standing in the community were more than he could bear, and he did the only thing he could think of—he ran to his father.

Winston Marshall looked at his son in disbelief when Thomas finished explaining the situation. "You risked everything—including the bank's reserves?"

When Thomas nodded, his father looked away in disgust.

"No son of mine could be that stupid. You are being groomed for political office for God's sake! What the deuce were you thinking?!" he thundered.

Thomas winced. "Morse said it was a sure thing. I thought it would put me on the inside track. What do I do, Father?" he whimpered. "If there is a run on the bank, I could go to jail."

"Well, I am not letting you bring disgrace upon this family for one thing. Stop sniveling. How much is the bank missing?"

Thomas took a deep breath. "Two hundred and fifty thousand."

"Two hundred and fifty thousand!" Winston Marshall let out an explosive expletive. Though he had plenty of assets, he didn't have nearly enough liquidity to cover his son's losses.

"Father, I—"

"Be quiet! I have to think."

A tense silence fell over the room. Thomas shifted his stance nervously as his father stared motionless out the window.

"Elizabeth's father left her bearer bonds," said the elder Marshall. "Are they in the bank?"

"Yes, in the vault," replied Thomas.

His father turned to him. "Then convince her to sign them over to you and cash them out. They must be worth over a million dollars."

"What do I tell her?"

"Well, you certainly don't tell her that you lost all your money and embezzled from the bank," snapped his father. "Tell her you want to invest the bonds for more security."

Thomas hesitated. "Elizabeth has been difficult lately. She's been getting foolish ideas in her head of going to school and marching in parades for women's rights. Dear God, she wanted to get a job!"

Winston Marshall gave a derisive snort. "These so-called modern women ought to be grateful that they have a roof over their heads."

"That's what I told her," said Thomas.

"Of course, it would help if you had children," remarked the elder Marshall, directing a pointed glance at his son. "Voters like to see a family. And children give a man leverage when his wife threatens to get out of line."

"Fine, but what do I do in the meantime if Elizabeth balks at handing over the bonds?" asked Thomas.

His father regarded him with a measure of exasperation. "Must I solve all your problems? She's your wife. Be firm of hand. Find something to leverage against her."

CHAPTER TWENTY-EIGHT

NO UPPER HAND

Elizabeth could sense that there was something different about her husband this night as they sat at the dinner table. He seemed preoccupied and, at times, she looked up to find him regarding her as though considering something.

"Is something wrong, Thomas?" she finally inquired.

"I've been thinking," he replied. "I think it time we begin a family in earnest."

Elizabeth stiffened. "I thought you weren't partial to children."

"A man needs progeny as part of his legacy."

"A man or a politician?" she quizzed sardonically.

Her husband ignored the pointed question. "A child would give you something to better occupy your time and mind, Elizabeth."

"A job would better occupy my time and mind," she retorted. "And I'll not have children for the purpose of serving as props, Thomas. Maybe you should have found a wife more suitable to your needs and ambitions."

Hard pressed to restrain his temper, Thomas moved to diffuse the contentious moment. He would need her in a better mood for his next proposal.

"We'll leave this discussion for another time," he said.

Elizabeth took a deep breath and closed her eyes in relief.

The maid entered, then, to clear away the meal and serve dessert and coffee. The interruption seemed to clear the air enough that Thomas felt comfortable broaching the more important subject.

"There have been some developments that have brought much uncertainty to the markets over the last several weeks," he began casually.

"Yes, I know," said Elizabeth. "I have been following the stories in the newspaper. There has been much mention of Mr. Morse and Mr. Heinze. They're the men you are so eager to embrace as your associates, are they not?" she asked, taking a sip of coffee.

"Uh…yes—that is they were. I no longer do business with them," he replied haltingly. "I wasn't aware you were reading the newspapers."

"Is it a crime?" she asked, feigning wide-eyed surprise.

Thomas bristled. "If you've been following the news, Elizabeth, then you are aware that it would be to your best interest to liquidate the bearer bonds that your father left you before money becomes too scarce. I shall make time tomorrow for you to come by the bank and sign the bonds."

"I'm afraid I can't do that, Thomas."

The rejection was like a slap across the face, and he recoiled in surprise. "I beg your pardon, madam?"

"The bonds are no longer in the bank, Thomas. They were removed two days ago," she replied.

Her husband stared at her in disbelief. "That's not possible. I would have been informed."

"When your bank accountant discovered reserves missing, he brought the bonds to me out of loyalty to my father," Elizabeth calmly explained. She took another sip of coffee. "He said that it is just a matter of time until your embezzlement is exposed."

Marshall was dumbfounded, and it was a moment until he found his voice. "That bastard!" he exclaimed. "I'll teach him to interfere in my business."

"I think you will find that Mr. Langtry has resigned and left town," said Elizabeth. "But he left me with a sworn statement regarding the missing funds as he feared being made the scapegoat."

"It proves nothing," retorted Marshall.

"It proves enough to send you to jail," she countered smoothly.

"You will be stained by the scandal as well, Elizabeth. Did you think of that?"

"I don't care, as long as I am free of you, Thomas."

Marshall clenched his jaw. "Where are the bonds, Elizabeth?"

She lifted her chin and squared her shoulders. "In a safe place where you will not find them. But I am prepared to sign over to you enough bonds to cover the missing reserves in exchange for a divorce."

"I've told you before, Elizabeth, divorce is out of the question. It is social and political suicide."

"So is going to jail for embezzlement, Thomas. Take your pick."

Thomas was shocked not only at the ultimatum, but that she had the nerve to serve him with one. His eyes narrowed. "You have changed, Elizabeth. You seem to think you have a say."

He stood up and circled her chair.

"You may think that you have the power to send me to jail, but you forget that my father—that I—have connections," he amended. "You, on the other hand, are a woman and have none since your father died."

He leaned down, his mouth close to her ear, his voice low. "Add to that, I have the means to send you someplace much worse, so do not try to bargain with me, dear wife. You will lose."

Elizabeth bristled and turned her head away from him. "Your threats carry no weight, Thomas. I will no longer be under your thumb."

He stood up. "Let us see about that, my dear."

Elizabeth watched with curiosity as Thomas left the room. She blanched when he returned with her journal.

"I think hearing that you converse with voices in your head will be enough to convince a judge that you would be better off in the Institute for Mental Illness," he said with a smug smile. "And, as you will be judged incapable, I shall assume full control over your affairs—including the bearer bonds."

Elizabeth felt the blood drain from her face. She had thought to finally have the upper hand. How could she have been so careless? Why had she been so stupid as to keep a journal in the first place? At the time, keeping a record of her strange experiences had served to make everything seem more real. Now it could be her undoing.

As her mind scrambled to come up with a response, she struggled to present a composed appearance. "Well then, it would seem that we are at an impasse," she remarked.

Thomas scoffed. "From where I sit, I hold all the cards, Elizabeth."

She lifted her eyes to him. "How badly do you need my bonds, Thomas?"

He snorted with impatience. "What is your point?"

"You will not find the bonds, and if anything happens to me, Mr. Langtry's statement will be sent to the state attorney's office and to local and state newspapers. They love this sort of scandal."

Elizabeth felt encouraged that she had hit a nerve when she saw his lips twitch.

"You may find a way to stay out of jail, but your political career will be over before it starts," she continued. "People tend not to vote for embezzlers—or husbands of crazy wives. That is my point, Thomas."

Her husband's features hardened. "Perhaps you should pay a visit to the Institute and see how well life in a mental hospital will suit you. Then we shall see who blinks first."

When Elizabeth remained stiff and silent, he went on. "You have three days to hand over the bearer bonds and Langtry's statement. Then, we shall engage in starting a family, and you shall play the dutiful wife and mother."

With that, he strode from the room.

Elizabeth looked down at the table, tears dropping onto her plate. "Please, Riley, come soon," she whispered.

CHAPTER TWENTY-NINE

BACK AND FORTH

Julia anxiously searched the park. When she spied Elizabeth sitting on a bench near the duck pond, she hurried over to her.

"Elizabeth, what has happened? You sounded so desperate in your note," she said, sitting down next to her friend.

"It's Thomas," replied Elizabeth, wiping away tears.

Julia searched her face. "Has he hurt you?"

Elizabeth shook her head and told Julia about the bearer bonds and Thomas' threat if she didn't give them to him. She left out mention of the journal.

Julia reacted with disgust. "What a snake that man is. How could Thomas possibly think he has the grounds to commit you? He is bluffing."

"He has connections through his father," Elizabeth reminded her. "I have made up my mind that I will not hand over my bearer bonds to him, Julia. I will place them in an anonymous trust to guarantee the future of Slaterville. A life with Thomas is no better than one spent in a mental institution."

"Elizabeth, have you ever seen one of those places? You cannot allow Thomas to put you in there. I couldn't bear it. There has to be another way."

Elizabeth thought for a moment. "Perhaps there is."

"What is it? How can I help?" asked Julia.

"Casually mention to your husband that you heard rumors there are irregularities occurring at Thomas' bank, that his accountant has resigned and left town in protest over it," instructed Elizabeth.

"Your husband and Thomas regard each other as competitors. If Lawrence begins to make inquiries, maybe Thomas will panic enough to take my offer—the bonds in exchange for a divorce."

Julia nodded. "Yes, that may work. Lawrence doesn't discriminate when an opportunity arises to sully a competitor. Leave it to me," she said with a wink.

* * * * *

The minute Dr. Garson walked in the door, Kip knew by the expression on his face that there was trouble.

"An Earth-directed CME has been detected," said Garson. "This is the one, gentlemen."

"How much time do we have?" asked Riley.

"Given the speed, NOAA calculates that it will arrive sometime next week," replied Garson. "We'll have to refine our search."

He pulled out his map and spread it across the table.

"If the mouth is being pulled toward Slaterville, we should concentrate our efforts here," he said, pointing to an area. "But there is a new worry."

Kip groaned. "What?"

"If the mouth is pulled too close to the one in the Slaterville grove, the wormhole may lose the time tunnel effect."

"So what do we do?" asked Kip.

Garson shook his head. "I don't know yet."

"David, how familiar are you with Dr. Tesla's experiments in Colorado Springs in 1899?" questioned Riley.

Garson thought for a moment. Then a smile spread across his features. "You are thinking about electrical resonance."

Riley nodded.

Kip heaved a sigh of impatience. "What are you talking about?"

"To attract the mouth of the wormhole and hold it in place, we need to pump negative ions into the area," explained Garson.

Kip snorted. "Well, that's clear as day. We don't even know where the damn thing is."

"We know that it is in this vicinity," said Garson. "There looks to be a clearing there. If we can increase the magnetic field here, the mouth will come to us."

"How?" asked Kip.

"By using lasers directed at solar panels to generate the power," replied Garson. He fell silent for a moment as he considered the matter. "We're going to need a very long ground rod to penetrate far enough into the Earth's surface. It might require a pile driver and time we don't have."

"Not to mention a permit," interjected Kip.

"If there were a well in the area…" mused Riley.

Garson sighed. "Even if there was, a residential well is too shallow."

"There's an abandoned gas well somewhere around there," recalled Kip. "The state pulled the permit when neighbors complained about contaminated ground water. It was a big story."

Garson brightened. "That's perfect! We can use the borehole. And the clearing is shielded from the road by trees and shrubs."

"Where are you going to get all this equipment?" asked Kip.

"I can get everything we need from the university labs," answered Garson. "The solar panels might be a bit tricky. We may have to borrow them."

Kip raised a brow. "Define the word 'borrow.' I'm not going to be a party to stealing, even in the interest of science."

"Not to worry," the professor assured him. "The university has fields of solar panels that are used in experiments. I don't think some panels will be missed for a few days."

This didn't comfort Kip, but he made no further comment.

Garson turned to Riley. "How many panels do you think we'll need?"

"We will have to determine the concentration ratio," said Riley. "I know well Tesla's coil and magnifying transmitter. But you will have to explain the laser and solar panel to me, David. Mr. Tesla envisioned harnessing solar rays for energy, so I understand the concept, but he wasn't able to find a way to collect and store the energy."

"Don't feel bad," said Kip. "It took over a hundred years for someone to figure it out."

As Garson launched into the physics behind laser technology and solar panels to an enthralled Riley, Kip made his way to the kitchen for a beer. When he returned, the two physicists were busily writing calculations on tablets of paper.

Kip sat down on the couch and turned on the television. A female anchor came on with breaking news.

"News Center has learned that a renowned physicist was found fatally shot this morning in his apartment in an apparent suicide. Dr. Amos Hamel was employed by a private company with government contracts and was working on a highly classified project for the military."

Garson suddenly stiffened. He dropped his pencil and rushed over to the television to listen to the rest of the report. A picture of the physicist came on the screen.

"According to colleagues, Dr. Hamel had become nervous and despondent when authorities sought to question him about missing classified documents. Further investigation into his background is raising questions about the credibility of his academic credentials and the efficacy of his work on this and other projects. But officials stress that national security has not been compromised."

"My God," murmured Garson.

Kip glanced at him in puzzlement. "Something wrong, Doc? You don't look so good."

Garson rushed back to the table and gathered up the calculations he and Riley had been working on. "I have to go to the university. I'll be back in a few days."

As he hurried out the door, Kip and Riley looked questioningly at each other.

CHAPTER THIRTY

THE MISSING PAGES

Stan Reingold, the head of university's physics department, wouldn't fit Kip's stereotypical image of a scientist—he was tall, thin, bald, clean shaven, and dressed in a dark suit.

"Stan, do you have a minute?" asked Garson, hovering in the doorway.

Reingold looked up from an overlarge desk strewn with papers and charts and smiled. "David, I thought you were on your way back to sunny California."

"Something has come up to keep me in the area longer," said Garson.

"Well, come in, come in. What can I do for you?"

Garson walked into a comfortable room of bookshelves filled with textbooks, studies, and academic journals, and a wall full of awards and diplomas.

"Stan, I need a favor."

"Sure, anything. I owe you," replied Reingold. "You bailed me out of a jam taking over Dr. Traynor's classes while he was on medical leave. And I'm hearing rave reviews from high school counselors on your lecture to their students during the science festival. What do you need?"

Garson handed him a sheet of paper. "I need to borrow everything on that list."

Reingold looked over the items. "That's a lot of power. What are you doing with it?"

"You could say that I'm conducting an experiment."

Reingold eyed Garson with skepticism. "I've known you a long time, David. You don't conduct experiments. You do mathematical equations. What are you up to?"

"If I told you, you wouldn't believe me, Stan."

Reingold leaned back in his ergonomic chair and folded his arms across his chest, his manner uncompromising. "You know you can't make a statement like that to a physicist and expect to be let off the hook. What's going on, David?"

Garson shut the door and sat down. "I found a wormhole, Stan."

Reingold stared at his old friend for a moment, then burst out laughing. "You always were a prankster, David. You almost had me there. What are you really up to?"

"This isn't a joke, Stan. I really found a wormhole that is acting like a time tunnel."

"You're serious."

Garson leaned forward in his chair. "I'm dead serious, Stan, and there's more."

Garson told his colleague the whole story. When he had finished, Reingold was speechless.

"If it were anyone other than you, David, I'd call security and have him run off the campus. A time traveler…what am I supposed to do with this?"

"Lend me the things on that list," said Garson.

"Yes…yes, of course—but on the condition that you take me with you. I have to see this for myself."

Garson smiled. "I was hoping you would say that. Riley and I could use your help setting up the magnetic field. The CME has picked up speed. There isn't much time."

The physicist paused, disturbed by another thought. "Stan, did you hear about Amos?"

Reingold sighed. "Yeah. It's all over the science community. Damn shame. He was brilliant in his field. Do you believe he committed suicide?"

Garson shook his head.

"Neither do I," said Reingold. "The hatchet job began too quickly. What the hell was Amos into, David? They say he stole classified information from the company he was working for."

"His employers trumped up the charge, Stan. The irony is that it's actually true. They just aren't aware of it yet."

Shock rolled across Reingold's features. "Amos really did steal classified information? How? He complained how closely employees were monitored."

"He had a photographic memory," replied Garson.

"Oh, right." Reingold shook his head in bewilderment. "It doesn't make sense. Amos of all people..." He looked at his colleague. "How do you know any of this?"

"Amos wrote everything down in longhand and sent it to me." Garson took out a manilla envelope from his briefcase. "It was forwarded from my office at Caltech."

Reingold's jaw dropped. "My God, David, you could be charged as an accessory to espionage! Why would Amos put you in such a position?"

"I'm sure it wasn't an easy decision for him," said Garson, "but he wanted someone to know the truth."

"What truth was worth his life?" Reingold paused with a thought. "Does this have anything to do with your time traveler?"

"Possibly," acknowledged Garson. "What's your evaluation of the last solar storm?"

"The numbers were weak. The storm shouldn't have been that strong, and the track was off," replied Reingold. "NOAA doesn't make those kinds of mistakes. It's clear something doesn't add up."

"Like maybe another energy source tapped into the shock wave of the corona mass ejection and supercharged it?" questioned Garson.

Reingold shrugged. "It would be a plausible explanation if it were possible."

"It's possible, Stan."

When Reingold gave a skeptical laugh, Garson held out the envelope. "See for yourself."

The physicist hesitated, but his curiosity as a scientist got the better of his fears of being charged as an accessory to espionage. He took the envelope and removed several lined sheets of tablet paper filled with hastily scribbled handwriting and formulas.

As Reingold read through them, he became more and more alarmed. "This is a black budget project. With the right corona mass ejection, whoever has this technology could increase the power of it enough to selectively knock out satellites and electrical grids."

He shook his head incredulous. "Amos' work revolved around developing and providing sustainable energy to the world. What was he thinking giving them this kind of technology? He knew what a group like this could do with it."

"Maybe he didn't know who he was working for," said Garson. "Or maybe when someone offers to fund your life's passion, you don't ask too many questions."

"David, if his employers don't know that he actually stole secrets, why did they kill him?"

"Maybe he started to ask too many questions," replied Garson.

Reingold ran a hand across his face considering the ramifications. "If word of this gets out—no wonder they didn't waste any time discrediting Amos. Which group do you think it is?"

"My guess would be MS16."

Reingold frowned, deeply concern. "Be careful, David. These guys don't mess around. If they find out you have these papers, you'll share Amos' fate."

* * * * *

Kip went out for a run to clear his head. Riley needed some quiet time to talk with Elizabeth. Dr. Garson and Dr. Yeshi had gone to the university, and Ericka was on duty at the hospital.

The cold, crisp air carried the scent of woodsmoke. For the first time in weeks, Kip felt grounded as he ran through the park seeing people go about their normal lives, and he stretched out the run, reluctant to return to that "other" world of suspended belief.

When he returned to the apartment, he collected his mail. There was a large, padded envelope among the bills. The return address was a law firm. That was never good news, and he hurried up the stairs. He walked into the apartment to find Riley sitting on the couch with his head in his hands.

"Is everything okay with Elizabeth?" he asked.

Riley looked up at him, his features drawn with worry. "She didn't say much, but I sensed that Thomas is becoming more threatening. Kip, what if I am too late to help her because the storms don't overlap at the right time? A miss of a day or even of a couple of hours could make the critical difference."

Kip didn't know what to say. He wanted to be supportive, but that scenario was a real possibility if, in fact, Riley was able to return at all—something he was still dubious about.

"I'm sorry, Riley. I don't have an answer for you. Just know we're all doing the best we can," said Kip. "That has to count for something in the cosmos. I can't believe that we've all been brought together like this for the purpose of failing."

Riley sighed. "Dr. Yeshe said much the same thing. I am sorry to burden you."

Kip put a hand on Riley's shoulder. "It's no burden. Keep the faith, my friend.... I'm going to take a shower and look through my mail."

Riley nodded. "Mind if I go for a walk? I know that you and Dr. Garson don't want me to see too much of the future."

"Have we been that obvious?"

"A little," replied Riley with a slight smile.

"Okay, go ahead, but don't stray too far. I don't want to have to call Detective Gillespie to search for you," joked Kip.

As Riley headed out the door, Kip went to his bedroom. He threw the mail on the dresser and undressed down to his skivvies. He was about to start into the bathroom for a shower when he noticed the padded envelope again.

He wavered for a second, then picked it up and tore it open. Inside was a thin box, five inches by seven inches, and a formal letter from an attorney introducing himself as the executor of Miss Madeleine Claymore's estate. The letter went on to say that Miss Claymore had left instructions for the enclosed item to be sent to Kip after her death.

Kip opened the box and found a framed photograph of a young Julia Trowbridge and Elizabeth Slater. A note was attached, which he assumed was from Maddie. It read: *A picture is worth a thousand words.* Kip stared at the photograph, his brows knit in puzzlement. Even from the grave, Maddie continued to confound him.

"What are you trying to tell me?" he wondered aloud.

If he had learned anything from the old girl, it was that things were seldom as they appeared—and that maybe a picture wasn't just a picture. Kip turned the frame over. The backing was of newspaper and sealed with Scotch tape. Neither looked old and dried; they were fairly recent. Carefully, he removed the backing, and pages of handwritten script fell out.

Kip picked them up and looked at them. His jaw dropped and his heart beat hard against his chest. They were the missing pages from Julia Trowbridge's diary. He sat down on the edge of the bed, all thoughts of a shower gone from mind as he started to read the entries and was drawn into a narrative he could never have imagined.

* * * * *

December 1, 1907

Julia Trowbridge opened the envelope and took out the folded piece of paper. Her brows were knit in perplexity as she read the note:

Meet me at the south side of the park as soon as possible in regards to Elizabeth. Immediacy is imperative. Come with discretion.

"Who gave you this note?" she asked the maid.

"A boy brought it to the door, Mrs. Trowbridge."

"Please take out my blue walking suit, Minnie."

"But you are due at a tea, madam," the maid reminded her.

"I have something else I must do. Tell the housekeeper to send my regrets. Say I have fallen ill. Then help me to dress."

"Yes, ma'am."

Inside of an hour, Julia crossed into the park and went to the south corner as instructed. This particular area was more wooded and secluded, and she suddenly felt nervous. Driven by her concern for Elizabeth, she had foolishly told no one where she was going.

"Mrs. Trowbridge."

Julia turned and her eyes widened in shock and disbelief when Riley Harrington stepped out from behind a tree. "My God," she breathed. "It is really you—in the flesh?" she asked, tentatively reaching out a hand to touch him.

Riley smiled. "A bit disheveled perhaps, but yes, it is I in the flesh."

"Everyone thought you dead." Julia's moment of incredulity gave way to anger. "Where have you been these past years? Why have you not contacted Elizabeth? Do you have any idea how much your disappearance has hurt her?"

"Yes, and I am truly sorry for it, but I had no choice."

Julia was not going to let him off the hook so easily. "What do you mean you had no choice?"

"I was gravely injured and woke up in a different place with amnesia. Now I am fully recovered and have come back for Elizabeth."

"She is married to Thomas Marshall now."

"I know."

"You know? How do you know?"

"That's not important. Does she love him?"

Julia hesitated. "No. She thinks only of you."

"Then I require you to take a message to her that I will be waiting for her at the train station this evening." He took out a pouch of coins and handed it to her. "Purchase two tickets and give them to Elizabeth."

"To where?"

"I don't care where. Someplace far away from here."

"Thomas won't give her a divorce, you know."

"We'll deal with that later," said Riley.

Julia was silent as she weighed her friend's chances for happiness with each man. It wasn't difficult to evaluate Elizabeth's life with Thomas. She was unquestionably miserable. But Julia was no more convinced that she would find contentment living as an adulterer with a man of little resources, however much she loved him.

"Elizabeth is accustomed to wealth, position, and luxury. What can you offer her?" Julia demanded to know.

Riley didn't flinch. "I can give Elizabeth a lifetime of love."

"Love can fade in the face of poverty, Mr. Harrington. Elizabeth has given away the bearer bonds her father left her so that Thomas can't claim them."

"And the soul can wither in the face of riches where there is no love," countered Riley. "On which do you think Elizabeth would choose to take her chances, Mrs. Trowbridge?"

Julia knew her friend well enough to know the answer to that. "All right, I will do as you ask, though I still am not convinced of the wisdom of it."

"Have no fear for Elizabeth, Mrs. Trowbridge. She may never be as wealthy as she is now, but I can provide adequately for her. I am not a man who lacks vision and ingenuity. I promise you, I will make her happy."

Julia nodded. "Where will you be in the meantime? You shouldn't wander around town. Someone might recognize you and alert Thomas."

"I will be careful," Riley assured her.

Meanwhile

Elizabeth awoke alternately filled with hope, doubt, and fear. Riley had told that her he was coming for her today. Was it true? Or was it a trick of the mind borne out of intense desire and desperation? She was afraid to know for certain for fear it would be the latter.

How could a sane mind consider such a thing to be possible—that a voice in her head that sounded like Riley could manifest itself into his person? And what did he mean when he said he was coming for her? A chill swept through her. He was supposed to be dead. Was she going to die and he was coming to escort her to heaven? Or had she been unwittingly conversing with a demon that was coming for her soul?

Such was Elizabeth's state of mind when Julia rushed unannounced into her bedroom in a high state of excitement.

"Where's Thomas?" she asked in a hushed voice.

"He's at the bank. Why? Julia, what has happened?" fretted Elizabeth.

Julia shut the door. "I've seen him," she said.

"Who?"

"Riley Harrington."

Elizabeth gasped. "It was really him—not a trick of the imagination or a spirit?"

Julia shook her head. "I touched him to make sure."

Tears welled up in Elizabeth's eyes, and she was giddy with joy and relief. Her friend was not given to flights of fantasy.

"Where...where did you see him?" she asked.

"In the park. He had sent me a note to meet him there," replied Julia. "Of course, I didn't know with whom I was meeting. I nearly fainted when I saw him. You are to meet him at the train station this evening."

A sob caught in Elizabeth's throat. "He said he would come for me."

Julia looked at her friend in surprise. "You have spoken with him? When?"

"It's a long story," said Elizabeth. "But the psychic at Violet's luncheon was correct."

Julia wrinkled her brow in bemusement. But there was no time to waste with questions.

"Pack a bag," she said. "I'll check it at the station for you when I purchase the train tickets. The ticket office was closed when I stopped by earlier. If you can get your hands on some money, you'll need that, too."

"Thomas keeps some money locked in his desk in the study," recalled Elizabeth, "but he keeps the key on his watch fob,".

Julia took a hairpin from her hair. "That's what these are for."

Elizabeth giggled. "Why, Julia, how larcenous you are. But I think Thomas has another key in his bureau. I'll get my bag."

Elizabeth checked the hall for servants. When the coast was clear, she hurried to the attic. Several minutes later, she returned with a large carpetbag. Julia helped her pack a change of clothes and some personal items.

"How are you going to sneak out of here?" asked Julia.

"Thomas usually goes to the club Thursday nights after an early dinner," replied Elizabeth. "If I wait until he leaves, I can get to the station by half past six."

"Just in case, you should have a story," said Julia. "There's an art exhibit at the museum tonight. Tell Thomas that you and I have plans to attend. I'll rent a cab and pick you up at six o'clock. When it drops us at the museum, you can take another cab to the station. It will be more difficult for Thomas to track you. Oh, and wear a hat with a veil."

Elizabeth giggled again. "I had no idea you were so gifted in the art of subterfuge." She hugged her friend. "Thank you, Julia. I shall miss you. I promise I will write, and you can come to visit when Riley and I are settled."

Julia picked up Elizabeth's bag. "You are sure about this?"

Elizabeth answered without hesitation. "Yes."

"You know what people will say about you," warned Julia. "You'll never be able to come home again."

Elizabeth nodded. "I know."

At dinner, Elizabeth worked hard to appear cool and composed. Maybe it was the nervous flutter inside her stomach that made her imagine that the air was more tense than usual, she thought.

"You keep looking at the clock, Elizabeth. Are you planning to go somewhere?" asked Thomas.

Elizabeth took a deep breath to steady herself. "Julia and I are going to the art exhibit at the museum tonight. I assume you will be going to your club."

He said nothing. Elizabeth lowered her eyes and concentrated on her food, conscious of his gaze on her.

"Trowbridge came to see me at the bank today," he said. "It seems that he heard a rumor that the bank was not sound and hinted at some illegalities. I wonder where he came by that?"

"I wouldn't know, Thomas."

"You don't lie very well, Elizabeth. Your little stunt to have Julia pass such information to her husband to force my hand was clever, but it didn't work. I managed to convince Trowbridge that Langtry was spreading false rumors because I fired him."

"The truth will come out, Thomas."

"Yes, but it has bought me enough time. Unfortunately, it has shortened your deadline, my dear. You now have until tomorrow morning to sign over the bearer bonds and Langtry's statement. Orderlies from the mental institution will arrive at 10 o'clock. It is up to you whether their trip will be in vain."

His manner was casual, but she knew it was no idle threat. She looked at him, her face devoid of expression. "I am done with this meal."

She stood up and left the dining room.

"Tomorrow morning, Elizabeth," he shouted after her.

Elizabeth tensely paced the floor of her bedroom, waiting for Julia to arrive. Finally, the clock struck the hour. A few minutes later, she heard the clip clop of horses' hooves as a cab pulled up in front of the house.

She quickly put on her coat, grabbed her hat, and hurried from the room. She was at the top of the stairs when she heard Thomas answer the knock on the door.

"Mrs. Trowbridge, Elizabeth has fallen ill. I'm sorry to say she won't be accompanying you to the museum this evening," he said.

Elizabeth's heart dropped, and she ran down the stairs.

"No! Julia, wait! Julia!" she cried out. But her husband had already closed the door and was barring the way. "How dare you!" she shouted.

He wrenched the hat from her hand. "Did you really think I wouldn't notice the money missing from my desk drawer, Elizabeth?" As she started to turn away from him, Thomas grabbed her arm. "Harrington is back, isn't he?"

She gave a derisive laugh. "Now, who is imagining things?"

Elizabeth gasped and nearly lost her footing when he slapped her hard across the face. Her husband had always been cold and cruel, but he had never struck her before.

Thomas took her by the shoulders and shook her. "He's here, isn't he? When there was no body, I suspected he might be alive. Those drunken fools couldn't do anything right."

Elizabeth pushed him away, and her eyes widened with a sudden realization. "My father didn't send those drifters after Riley. You did."

Thomas scoffed. "I knew Harrington wouldn't believe you had changed your mind when your father kept you from meeting him that night, and he would continue to be a problem. I told your father he would have to be more direct, but he didn't see the need. So, I had to take matters into my own hands."

Elizabeth looked at her husband in disbelief. "All this time you let me blame my father? You really are a monster."

"You wanted a reason not to forgive him, Elizabeth. I gave it to you. I've been waiting for Harrington to come back. I didn't think it would take him four years. Where is he? Where were you to meet him?"

When Elizabeth didn't answer, he took her roughly by the arm and propelled her into the drawing room. "Have it your way," he said, shoving her roughly onto the sofa. "We can sit here all night. I have nowhere to be."

Elizabeth looked at the clock, blinking back tears. Her chance for happiness was ticking away for yet a second time.

Meanwhile

"Hurry!" Julia shouted to the driver. "I must get to the railroad station."

"If I go any faster, miss, we'll not make it at all."

"If you don't go faster, I'll drive this thing myself!"

Conscious of the importance of his passenger, the driver picked up the pace. Still, it seemed an eternity until the cab pulled up at the station. It had barely come to a stop before Julia jumped out of the conveyance and ran over to where Riley was waiting.

"Where's Elizabeth?" he asked, looking around for her.

"Thomas won't let her leave the house," said Julia, stopping to catch her breath. "Somehow he knows."

"Did you get the tickets?"

"No. The ticket window was still closed. You'll have to get on a train and pay the conductor."

She started to pull out the pouch of coins from her purse to return it to him, but Riley was already hurrying toward the cab.

"Where are you going?" she asked, running after him.

"I'm going after Elizabeth. No one is going to interfere this time."

The driver looked down when Riley rushed up to him. "You appear to be in a hurry, son. Where do you want to go?"

"I have need of your cab, sir," said Riley. "Please step down."

"What's that?" asked the driver in surprise.

"I don't have time to explain. It will be returned to you." He pulled the startled driver from the seat and climbed up to take his place.

"Wait, I'm coming, too," said Julia, yanking open the door and jumping inside the cab.

Riley didn't have time to argue and slapped the reins. The driver stared after them, stunned, as his cab disappeared from view.

As Riley raced through the streets weaving in and around cabs, carriages, and pedestrians, a wide-eyed Julia braced herself and clung to her seat for dear life. She caught herself from being thrown forward just in time when the cab came to an abrupt halt outside the Marshall house.

Riley jumped down from the seat. "Stay here," he shouted to her.

Julia watched in astonishment as he ran up to the door, kicked it open, and disappeared inside.

"Elizabeth!" shouted Riley. "Elizabeth!"

Thomas and Elizabeth immediately appeared from the drawing room and stared at him, incredulous. After all these years, neither could believe they were actually seeing him.

"Riley," murmured Elizabeth, choking back tears. She started to run to him, but Marshall grabbed hold of her.

"She's not coming with you this time either, Harrington."

Riley turned a cold eye on him. "Why don't we let Elizabeth decide that?" He looked at her. "Elizabeth, do you want to stay here with him or come away with me?"

"I want to go with you," she said. She tried to break free of her husband, but he increased the pressure of his hand on her arm.

"Let go of her," warned Riley.

"She is my wife. She is not going anywhere with you, Harrington."

"I'm not leaving without her, Marshall."

"Well, what do you think you are going to do about it?" jeered Thomas.

Riley responded with a hard right cross to Thomas' jaw and laid him out on the floor before he knew what had hit him. Elizabeth ran into Riley's arms, and he hustled her out to the cab.

Julia opened the door and pulled her inside.

"Hurry or you're going to miss the next train," she said.

Riley slammed the door shut and climbed up on the seat. He turned the cab around, and it lurched forward as he whipped the horse into a run.

The theater was just letting out and traffic had picked up. Riley chafed at the delay. They finally pulled up at the station just as the whistle blew to announce the train's departure in five minutes. Riley jumped down from the driver's seat and helped the women out of the cab.

"I'll get Elizabeth's bag," said Julia.

"We don't have time." He took Elizabeth's hand and started toward the passenger car.

"Wait!" exclaimed Julia. She pointed to several policemen who were stopping passengers attempting to board the train. "Let me find out what it's about."

Riley nodded and pulled Elizabeth into the shadows with him.

Several minutes later, Julia returned.

"Thomas notified the police that Elizabeth has been kidnapped and that he has reason to believe the kidnapper is taking her away by train," she reported. "They're searching all the passenger cars too."

Elizabeth gripped Riley's arm. "There's Thomas."

Riley turned to see Marshall riding up on a horse and approach a policeman. Even from this distance, Elizabeth could see that he was in a rage.

"He is never going to let me go, Riley," she whispered dispiritedly. "He won't rest until he finds us and hurts you. I have to go back."

"I think she is right," said Julia. "Thomas can be very vindictive, and he has resources. His father is well connected."

Suddenly, a bright display of green, purple, and pink ribbons of light lit up the sky—the second and most brilliant of the week that illuminated even areas normally in shadow. All motion stopped as everyone paused what he was doing to stare up at the astounding show.

"The aurora borealis," murmured Riley. He turned to Elizabeth. "You're not going back. Get into the cab. There may be another way. Mrs. Trowbridge, I'm sorry, but you'll have to get another cab to take you home."

Julia shook her head, adamant in her resolve. "I'm not leaving Elizabeth until I know she is safe."

The women climbed back into the cab, and Riley retook the driver's seat. He had just turned the conveyance around, when there came a shout and the sound of police whistles. Elizabeth twisted around to see her husband mounting his horse and policemen running in pursuit of them.

"Riley, hurry! Thomas is coming after us."

"Hold on," he shouted to the women.

He whipped the horse, and Elizabeth and Julia held on as they sped down the main road and rounded the curve practically on two wheels. Riley looked over his shoulder to see that Marshall was close behind them. He had to stay ahead of the man for a few more miles.

Finally, the grove came into view, and Riley drove several yards into it before bringing the horse to a stop.

He jumped from his seat and yanked open the door. "Elizabeth, come with me."

He helped her out of the carriage and, holding her hand in a tight grasp, ran toward a strange swirling light visible just above the ground. As they got closer, what looked like bolts of lightning flashed all around them. The ground vibrated beneath their feet and the air crackled with electricity.

She pulled back. "Riley, what is this?" she cried, fearful.

"Elizabeth, do you trust me?"

Elizabeth looked over her shoulder to see her husband galloping into the grove. He was dismounting and running toward them. She looked from the light to Riley. "Yes," she said.

He put his arms around her. "Hold onto me and don't let go," he instructed.

Marshall shouted for them to stop. He raised a gun and fired point blank just as they disappeared into the light.

Standing outside the cab, Julia stared in disbelief. A paddy wagon had arrived on the scene minutes before, and the policeman sat frozen in his seat. Four other policemen, one a sergeant, rode in then.

Marshall began screaming that his wife was inside the still glowing light. He started to run up to it, but the ground was so charged he stopped. The horses nervously pranced and whinnied struggling to break free. Marshall's horse had already galloped off.

"Pull the horses back before they all run off," ordered the sergeant. "Someone tend to Mr. Marshall."

Julia followed after a policeman as he led the skittish horse that was harnessed to her cab to the road. When everyone had congregated and the horses were more settled, the sergeant approached Julia. "What went on here?"

"I don't know," she said. "I think there was a huge lightning strike."

The officer looked at the driver of the paddy wagon. "Whitley, what did you see?"

James Whitley hesitated and looked at Julia. "I-I think the lady is correct, sir," he stammered. "There was a very large lightning strike."

"Sergeant Calhoun, strange things have been happening with the telegraph this week," commented another policeman. "Something about solar flares. It has been in the paper, sir. That's why the strange lights in the sky Tuesday night and tonight."

The sergeant turned back to Julia. "Where is Mrs. Marshall? Her husband is beside himself. He claims she was kidnapped and brought here."

"I haven't seen Mrs. Marshall since this morning," replied Julia. "We were supposed to attend an art exhibit at the museum this evening, but when I arrived to pick her up, her husband told me she was ill and would not be attending. He was quite angry. I think they had been quarreling."

"What are you doing here alone in the grove, madam, and where is the driver of this cab?" He looked at his officer. "Is this the cab that was reported stolen, Massey?"

"I'm sorry, Sergeant," said Julia. "As I was leaving the museum, Mr. Marshall came tearing past on his horse shouting Elizabeth's name. He appeared quite unhinged. And fearing for my dear friend's safety, I felt it imperative to follow after him. I found a cab but no cabman, so I borrowed the carriage."

"I don't care what you call it, lady. Do you know what the jail time is for this?"

"Ah, Sergeant, I believe this is Mrs. Trowbridge," Massey informed his superior in a lowered tone.

The sergeant looked at the officer sharply. "Are you sure?"

Massey nodded, and the sergeant swallowed hard. "My pardons, Mrs. Trowbridge. I'm sure the matter of the cab can be put to rest without any undue notice. Do you know why Mr. Marshall came to the grove?" he inquired in a more courteous tone.

"No, sir, none at all. I heard him say something about Elizabeth not being able to escape him," Julia added with seeming innocence. "She told me that Mr. Marshall had become quite abusive towards her of late. May I go now, Sergeant? I am feeling quite distressed."

"Of course, Mrs. Trowbridge. I shall have an officer see you home."

Julia took out a handkerchief and dabbed fake tears from her eyes. "Please check on my friend, Sergeant. I am quite worried for her."

The sergeant nodded. As he walked away with the policeman, he instructed him, "Keep this quiet, Massey, but make a note in your report that Marshall was found in a state of hysteria and incoherency and appeared to have been drinking. Let someone else sort this out."

"Anything else, sir?"

"Send someone to the Marshall house to see if Mrs. Marshall is there."

"And if she isn't?"

"Talk to the servants and get some men out here to search the grove."

"Do you think Marshall might have done away with his wife, sir?" asked Massey.

"I don't know. But if she is found to be missing and no body is located, I'm not getting sucked into the circus when that Harrington fellow disappeared…and I don't think the prosecutor will want to, either. The town can pass its own judgment."

* * * * *

Kip finished reading the last page of Julia Trowbridge's account. The page slipped from his fingers and fluttered to the floor as he stared off into space. What the hell—

He suddenly stood up from the bed and rushed into the living room. "Riley!" he shouted.

When silence met his ears, thoughts ricocheted around his brain like a pin ball. Had it all been some kind of a dream? Had he imagined everything? Had he lost his mind? Was he caught up in some cosmic joke?

Riley walked through the front door then. His brow drew together in bemusement as Kip stared at him as though seeing a ghost. "Are you all right?" he asked. "Is something wrong?"

Kip mentally shook himself. "Uh, no. Look, I have to go out for a while. Will you be okay alone?"

"Of course. I don't need babysitting," said Riley. "But maybe you should get dressed first," he quipped.

Kip glanced down at his skivvies. "Uh…right. I was getting ready to get a shower, when—never mind."

He hurried back to his bedroom to get dressed.

CHAPTER THIRTY-ONE

A BIGGER STORY

Garson was on his way to Kip's apartment when he received Kip's call that they meet at the coffee house. Clearly, something had rattled him. The professor could hear it in his voice.

Garson walked into the coffee house and slid into the booth across from Kip. "What's up? Why did we have to meet here instead of at the apartment?" he asked.

Kip shoved pages filled with early 20th century style script in front of him. "They're the missing entries from Julia Trowbridge's diary. You need to read them."

Garson picked up the pages. "Where did you find them?"

"They came in the morning mail—from the grave you might say."

As the physicist read through them, the expression on his face changed from bewilderment to disbelief. When he laid down the last page, his manner was solemn.

Kip did not find this comforting. He tapped the diary pages on the table. "What the hell does this mean, David? According to this account, Riley had already returned to Slaterville in 1907, and he and Elizabeth disappeared together. So why is Riley here now? Where is Elizabeth?"

Garson looked at him. "It means we have more of a problem than we thought."

"Jesus, what now?!" exploded Kip. "What kind of a problem?"

Garson hesitated to say knowing this was not going to land well. "Did you ever hear of parallel worlds or multi-universes?" he asked.

"Anyone who has ever read science fiction or watched a sci-fi movie knows about them," Kip responded impatiently. "What's this have to do with Riley?"

"Within the quantum concept of parallel universes, there is the theory of Many Worlds. It states that the universe splits into different realities when there is the possibility of more than one outcome to an action," explained Garson. "Proponents call it the splintering of the universe.

"Scientists have been debating the premise for decades. The problem has been that there is no good way to irrefutably prove or disprove it," he went on. "Riley may be the proof scientists have been seeking."

Kip leaned forward. "Are you telling me this isn't just a time travel event…that I'm in some friggin' alternate reality?"

"Not exactly," said Garson.

"What exactly the hell is it then?!" erupted Kip.

Garson glanced at the patrons around them. "Keep your voice down…. Something occurred that created a temporal distortion or a warping of the fabric of space-time."

"English, Doc."

"Whatever anomaly happened, it caused the events in the grove in 1903 to be repeated, creating another outcome or history," said Garson. "But instead of our world splitting off a completely separate reality to accommodate it—as the theory holds—I believe the alternate reality has somehow remained attached to our world."

Kip put his head in his hands at the breaking point. "So, what are you saying—there are two Riley Harrington's in our world?"

Garson nodded. "Yes."

Kip looked up at him. "I was joking."

"I'm sorry, but it's the only thing that makes sense," said Garson.

"Nothing has made sense since I found Riley, Doc."

Kip paused with a sudden thought. "Maddie Claymore said there were two histories, that the universe was out of balance. I thought she was nuts or senile. She said I was chasing a bigger story than I knew. When I asked her what it was, she said I would have to discover the facts myself or I wouldn't believe them."

Kip raked a hand through his hair. "Jesus, she was right. I'm hard pressed to believe them now."

Garson gave him a sympathetic smile. "If it makes you feel any better, scientists are still grappling with these concepts."

"Where are the other Riley and Elizabeth?" asked Kip.

The physicist sighed. "They could be anywhere, in any decade. Then there's the possibility they didn't survive the wormhole, but we can't take that chance. Riley must be returned to his own time to fuse the histories."

"What if we aren't successful?" asked Kip.

"Then there will be more than just a ripple effect," replied Garson with stark sobriety. "Our world will contain dual realities without the natural barriers and order to things. There will be nothing to keep the two realities from bleeding into each other."

"Meaning?" pressed Kip.

"It could set up a doppelganger effect and create unimaginable confusion and chaos," replied Garson. "Riley has been here two months. It's probably already happening."

Kip stared at Garson, incredulous. "There are two of me, two of you, two of everyone in this world?"

"Not of everyone, but those affected will be unintentionally crossing back and forth into each other's realities just by walking out the front door or driving down the street," said Garson.

"Christ Almighty." Kip raked a hand through his hair again. "If you're right, why haven't we heard something about it?"

"There may be a few posts on some fringe internet sites now," replied Garson. "Over time, others will follow, but most won't ever speak of their encounters. No one wants to be thought crazy."

Kip gave a humorless laugh. "I can identify with that. You said Riley has to be returned to the same life to fuse the two histories. That means he'll have to do everything the same. How will this Riley know what the other Riley did? He could do something different and nothing will be resolved."

"Events will lead him," said Garson.

"How do you know?" pressed Kip.

"Riley is still Riley. The circumstances will be the same, and his thought processes will be the same in response to them."

"Maybe he should read the diary," suggested Kip.

Garson shook his head. "I don't think that is a good idea. He may be tempted to do something that circumvents an action."

Kip fell silent, the knot in his stomach tightening. The friggin' goal posts just kept moving.

"Doc, this space-time distortion thing…how did it occur?" he asked.

Garson shrugged. "It happens sometimes. People have been seeing doppelgangers and experiencing strange things all through time. But balance is always restored, and events are relegated to the realm of the unexplainable."

The physicist paused for a moment debating how much more to lay on Kip and decided that he needed to know everything for his own protection.

"Kip, this time, I believe there was another source of electromagnetic energy generated that intensified the solar storm in the upper stratosphere to the point that it created this distortion…. I think it was part of an experiment."

Kip looked at Garson in disbelief. "Someone did this intentionally? Who…NASA?"

Garson shook his head. "A black budget group. I think the anomaly they created was unanticipated."

Unanticipated! Kip seethed with anger. His belief system, his sense of reality and his place in it were totally screwed up because of a damned experiment?!

"Do these bastards realize what they've done?!"

"Probably not yet, but they understand they have significantly impacted Earth's electromagnetic fields," replied Garson.

"They'll be closely monitoring for any anomalies. When they start to see postings on YouTube, they'll take steps to make sure mainstream media ignore the stories," he went on to explain. "Those people who persist in trying to make their stories known will be marginalized in the way ufologists have been for decades."

"Then, what's to keep this group from creating a distortion again?" Kip demanded to know.

"Well, scientists the world over abhor a mystery," answered Garson. "They're already asking questions and will figure it out. Of course, the group responsible will deny everything, and no one will be able to prove anything, but the scientific community will know, and world governments will keep a close eye on the group's activities."

Kip pushed his coffee away. "I think I need something stronger. Excuse me." He reached for his coat to leave.

"Kip, we need to keep this between us," warned Garson. "If these people find out about Riley, they'll take custody of him, and by the time they figure out what we have figured out, the window to send him back will have closed."

"Doc, really?"

"I'm serious, Kip. There are no lengths to which they will go to protect themselves. If word of this distortion gets out before they have time to cover their tracks, there will be an uproar of gigantic proportions in the scientific and geopolitical world. They'll take no chances."

"Are we talking helicopters and men in black suits?" remarked Kip with heavy sarcasm.

"I know how paranoid this sounds, but these people can destroy you, Kip, and you'll never see it coming," warned Garson. "It happened to a friend and colleague of mine, a highly regarded physicist in his field."

Kip settled back down in the booth. "What happened to him?"

"They discredited him, erased his credentials from the record, saw him charged him with stealing classified information." Garson paused, visibly affected. "Amos recently committed suicide—or so that's the way it was made to appear."

"Wait a minute," said Kip. "Are you talking about that guy who was in the news?"

Garson nodded.

Kip let out a low whistle. "No wonder you were so upset when you left the other day. You don't believe he committed suicide?"

Garson shook his head.

"How do you know he was murdered?"

"This isn't the first time it has happened," replied Garson. "It's their M.O. These are dangerous people, Kip. They control the flow of information. They write the script for this stuff. No one goes rogue. No one talks out of school without suffering the consequences."

It was a popular theme with conspiracy groups whose members Kip had dismissed as nut cases. But Dr. Garson had credentials. He couldn't be so easily dismissed.

"What about NASA—the portals it has discovered and the MMS project?" questioned Kip. "It doesn't sound as though they're being controlled by an outside group."

"The MMS project has been delayed another year due to more 'budget cuts,'" replied Garson. "Congress may hold the purse, but these groups pull the strings, and they can be subtle—or not. Do you think it was by chance that a science-denier was chosen to chair the senate oversight committee on NASA?"

Kip had to admit that the choice had risen to the level of absurdity.

"It was a shot across the bow of NASA not to overstep," said Garson. "I suspect the director ran afoul when he announced the findings of the portals and the MMS project to study them."

He leveled a steady eye on Kip. "Watch yourself. Be careful what you say and to whom. The reach of these people is long and deep."

His warning penetrated.

Kip froze with a sudden thought. "Doc, after I found Riley, I had the newspaper run his picture and a story in hopes that someone could identify him. Do you think these guys might have picked up on that?"

"Did you post anything on the internet?" quizzed Garson.

Kip shook his head. "I didn't get that far."

"How much did you disclose in the newspaper about him?"

"Just that Riley was found along the road, injured and unconscious, dressed in period clothes—and that he had amnesia," replied Kip. "Ericka asked me not to write any more stories about him until we knew what had happened. Then, it became a moot point."

"If no one has been around asking questions by now, your article probably escaped notice," said Garson. "But remain vigilant just the same."

For the next few days, Kip was on edge, looking over his shoulder for "men in black" and fearing that every time he walked out the door, he might find himself in an alternate reality. Elongated shadows in the evening menaced, the dark of night pulsated danger.

Ericka stopped coming around. Kip was glad about that. The last thing he needed right now was to be probed by a skeptical psychiatrist dealing with her own crisis of science.

Riley was too focused on finding his way back to Elizabeth to notice Kip's tense demeanor, but Dr. Yeshe noticed and suggested that Kip learn to meditate to relax. Kip wanted to laugh. How does one relax in the face of crossed dimensions and doppelgangers?

CHAPTER THIRTY-TWO

THE MOMENT IS AT HAND

Ericka walked out of the hospital, and her step faltered when she saw Kip leaning against his car waiting for her. She took a deep breath and walked up to him.

"What are you doing here? Did we have a coffee date or something?" she asked.

"Nope," said Kip.

Ericka looked away. "I can't help you search for the wormhole anymore, Kip. It's just too antithetical to—I need more time."

Kip smiled. "It's not about that either. I thought you might want to be present for this."

Her gaze swiveled back to him. "Present for what?"

"Have you heard about the approaching solar storm?"

Ericka shook her head. "I've been busy. I haven't paid much attention to the news."

"Dr. Garson says it's the one we've been watching for. He has calculated that the mouth of the wormhole should be opening sometime in the next 24 hours."

Ericka puckered her brow in bemusement. "Are you saying you found it?"

Kip grinned. "We did. Actually, you could say it found us."

Ericka's eyes widened in astonishment. "How?"

He explained how Riley, the professor, and a colleague of Garson from the university created a magnetic field to draw the mouth of the wormhole to them. He refrained from freaking her out with alternate realities and "men in black."

Ericka shook her head. "I can't believe it's real," she murmured.

"If you're game, you should change into something more comfortable," advised Kip. "It's going to be an around-the-clock stakeout. I have blankets, drinks, and snacks in the trunk."

She hesitated for a moment. "I'm supposed to be a woman of science. I am bound to see where this goes," she decided.

Kip followed her home and waited in the car while she changed clothes. Fifteen minutes later, she returned and settled into the front seat.

"Last chance to turn back," he said. "You'll either feel like a fool, or you'll have your whole world turned upside down."

"I've already had it turned upside down," she responded. "For the first time in my life, I envy my sister. Patty wouldn't have a problem with any of this." Ericka reached for the seat belt. "Let's go."

When they drove up to the spot, Kip pulled off the road and followed a path into a clearing. Ericka let out a gasp of surprise at the sight of a vast array of solar panels hooked up to a laser and the bank of batteries and capacitors with lines running to a rod driven deep into the borehole of the abandoned well. Riley, Dr. Garson, and another man roamed the field, double-checking the apparatus and the connections.

Kip was amused by her reaction. "It looks like something out of a cheap sci-fi flick, doesn't it?"

"What is all of this? What are they doing?" asked Ericka, wide-eyed.

"They're increasing the magnetism in the ground to hold the wormhole in place," explained Kip. "That's Dr. Reingold there from the university who lent us the equipment."

Dr. Yeshe approached them.

"And how does a psychiatrist view this event, Dr. Porter?" the Buddhist monk asked her with a twinkle in his eye.

Ericka gave him a crooked smile. "I'm not quite certain," she replied.

"The journey can be long or short as one desires it, Doctor."

Kip took out a battery-powered radio and turned it on. A news bulletin was just being announced, and he waved to the other men to gather around.

"A coronal mass ejection is nearing Earth at over 1,000 miles a second, creating a shock passage that is expected to intensify an already strong solar storm. At this rate of speed, the CME is due to arrive in the early morning hours..."

"When will the mouth open?" asked Kip.

"When there's maximum disruption from the shock wave. No way to say exactly," said Garson. "We must watch for electrical discharges and a light around the edge of the mouth."

"It will have the appearance of a Tesla coil," interjected Riley.

"What do we do in the meantime?" asked Ericka.

"We wait," said Garson. He turned to Kip. "Do you have clothes for Riley?"

Kip nodded. "In my car. The guy at the costume store assured me the style was authentic to the period."

"Elizabeth said a faint borealis has been visible for two days. Maximum electromagnetic disruption should occur in a few hours there. How long will the mouth stay open on that end?" asked Riley.

"There were two solar storms back-to-back in 1907. You should have at least 24 hours," said Garson.

"That means maximum intensity must occur here within that window," noted Dr. Yeshe.

"Yes, but I have calculated that we need an overlap of only an hour." Garson looked at Riley. "We have done our best calculations, young man. Still, there is no telling what can happen," he cautioned.

Riley nodded. "I understand, but I have to take the risk. Elizabeth is waiting for me."

The man has no idea what is resting on his shoulders, thought Kip. He took Garson aside. "What if these black budget people try their experiment again?"

"I don't think they would take that chance this soon," said Garson. "Their scientists are most likely still assessing if there was any fallout from the first event."

The hours dragged by slowly. Everyone was tense.

Riley changed into his period clothes and went off by himself to communicate with Elizabeth one last time.

"I don't know if you hear me, my dearest Liza, but if all goes well, I will see you tomorrow," he said.

His words were muffled by the disruption of the upper atmosphere magnetic fields, but Elizabeth did hear them, and she gathered them to her heart.

"Godspeed," she whispered.

CHAPTER THIRTY-THREE

MUM IS THE WORD

It was just before dawn when Kip's radio and cell phone stopped working. He tried to pull up something on his iPad, but the satellites were down.

"We must be watchful now," said Garson.

A few hours later, Kip felt the tingling sensation he had felt in the grove. "Do you feel that?" he asked.

Ericka moved closer to him. "Yes. What is it?"

"It's the shock wave affecting the electromagnetic fields," said Garson. "The feeling will intensify as the corona mass ejection comes closer."

As he had predicted, the tingling increased over the next three hours until the air seemed to crackle with energy. Garson measured the radiation. "I think we should move nearer to the mouth now."

He ran the EMF meter over the area. "Here," he said, pointing to a spot, "I believe this to be the opening."

Just then, Detective Gillespie came roaring onto the field in his squad car. Kip groaned and moved to intercept him.

"Stevens! I should have known you would be involved somehow," the detective blustered as he got out of the car.

Kip struggled to keep his cool. "What are you doing here, Hank?"

"Reports came into the station that something was going on in this field," grumbled Gillespie. "People were worried it might be kids doing some kind of satanic ritual."

The detective looked around at the display of solar panels, capacitors, and batteries in amazement. "What the hell is this? Who are these people? What's John Doe doing here?"

"Dr. Garson and Dr. Reingold are from the university and are conducting an experiment," replied Kip, thinking quickly. "Dr. Porter is John's psychiatrist. She thought it would be a good idea for John to help with the experiment, since he appears to have a scientific background. It might jog his memory."

"What kind of experiment?" the detective demanded to know.

Kip followed on his heels as he moved closer to the action.

"They're measuring the Earth's magnetic field in the wake of a solar flare," he explained. "You've heard the news reports about the geomagnetic storm, haven't you?"

Gillespie snorted. "Of course, I have. The damn comms went down again. What's with these storms all of a sudden?"

"The sunspot cycle is in solar maximum," said Kip.

The detective looked at him blankly. "You know something, Stevens, you've been hangin' out with eggheads too much. Do these guys have a permit?"

"You know eggheads," replied Kip. "They're by the book. You had better go now, Hank, before you contaminate the experiment."

He started to usher the detective back to the squad car when the cells on the solar panels suddenly began to explode.

Gillespie stopped and turned back. "What the—"

He did a dance as a strong electric current ran underground beneath his feet. "Stevens, what the hell is going on?"

Enormous jags of lightning leaped across the area then, and a brilliant, swirling light appeared a few feet above the ground, growing larger.

Gillespie stared open-mouthed at it. "What—what is that!"

"The opening of a wormhole," replied Kip in wonderment.

"I think this is my cue," said Riley.

"You were unconscious when you came through the first time, so you don't know what to expect. Try to relax and let the energy carry you," counseled Garson. "Don't fight it."

Riley nodded.

Kip took the pouch of silver coins from his jacket pocket, realizing now the significance of the coins. "You're going to need some money," he said, handing Riley the small leather bag. He took off his watch. "It isn't one of those fancy ones so it shouldn't get you into trouble, but I'd like you to have it. Give my best to Elizabeth."

Riley put a hand on Kip's shoulder. "You have been a good friend. I shall miss you. I don't know what will happen, but I will send you a message if I can."

He quickly made his farewells to everyone and walked to the light. In the next instant, he was sucked into the energy vortex.

No one said anything for several minutes. Then Dr. Yeshe closed his eyes and murmured a prayer. Mesmerized, Kip stepped closer to the wormhole.

"Careful," said Garson. "The mouth is still open."

"My God," breathed Reingold. "Do you think Riley made it?"

"Only time will tell," responded Garson soberly.

Kip looked at Ericka. "Do you still believe that coincidence can't be fate?"

"I think now that fate can be coincidence with a higher purpose," she responded solemnly.

Gillespie ran a hand over his head. "Wh-what the hell just happened?" he sputtered, dazed. "Where's John Doe?"

"Hopefully, in 1907 Slaterville," replied Kip.

Gillespie stared at him flabbergasted, his toupee askew. "Are you telling me this guy really was a friggin' time traveler?"

"You saw the ballistics test and the clothing he was found wearing, Hank. What do you think? Were you able to prove the evidence box was faked?"

The detective gazed around at the others and backed away from them.

"I don't know what this was tonight, but it didn't happen, Stevens. Do you understand me? I don't want to read a word about this in the newspaper. All of you—this didn't happen!"

He turned and ran to the squad car. Dirt flew as he sped out of the clearing.

"He's right," said Garson. "None of us can speak of this. The world isn't ready for it yet."

"Don't worry. No one will hear anything from me," Ericka was quick to assure him.

They were all exhausted, every manner of emotion running through them. Kip helped Garson and Reingold load the solar panels and equipment unto the truck, then dropped Ericka at her home and Dr. Yeshe at his hotel. By the time he walked into his apartment, it was after noon.

He felt the emptiness right away as he wandered through the rooms. It was as though nothing had happened and yet it did. Everything about his life would seem trivial now, and he didn't know if he could get used to that. His sense of wonder would never be the same.

His thoughts went to Riley. Had he made it back to the right place at the right time? Was he with Elizabeth? Were the two histories now reconciled? Only time would tell. But there was another question loomed large for him that had gotten lost in all the detail. What had happened to the Elizabeth and Riley who had entered the wormhole in 1907 Slaterville?

The next morning, Kip went to the newspaper office. He needed that degree of normalcy in his life—the kind of ignorance-is-bliss normalcy. He didn't care if what he considered to be reality was an illusion so long as it was his illusion. He didn't want to think about alternate worlds, crazy science, wormholes or shadowy government groups. He just wanted to be Kip Stevens, journalist, and spend his free time convincing Ericka Porter that he was a great guy.

When he entered the editorial room, his editor looked at him in surprise. "Wondered if you were coming back. I thought maybe you had gone back to the big city where there's more excitement."

Kip smiled. "I find excitement enough here. A source tells me there is some question about Councilman Warren's campaign funding. I want the assignment."

"Jack is covering City Hall now."

Kip snorted. "Jack wouldn't know a red herring if one jumped into his lap."

Dittmore grinned. "Welcome back, Stevens. You were missed around here. And if you quote me on that, I'll deny it. Whatever happened to the John Doe story you wasted so much of my time and resources on?"

"It's not going to pan out," said Kip.

"Why not? Has he remembered his name yet?"

Kip hesitated. "He has."

"Who is he then?"

"Well, he says he's Riley Harrington."

Dittmore was taken aback. "The man from 1903?" He eyed Kip with suspicion. "You haven't been drinking again, have you?"

"I'm as sober as you, Chief."

The editor pulled on his chin. "Well, then, the guy is either crazy or pulling some stunt. Still it's a strange story. Keep it in the stack in case there are more developments…. And tell Jack you're covering City Hall again."

Kip went to his desk and sat down. He leaned back in his chair and locked his hands behind his head. A smile spread across his features. Everything felt normal now, and he reveled in the feeling for a few minutes more before opening his computer and getting to work.

By the end of the day, he was fully and happily operating in his realm of delusion. He called Ericka, and she agreed to meet him for dinner with one ground rule. No discussion about wormholes and time travel. Kip was fine with that.

EPILOGUE

Kip finished his article and was preparing to leave the newsroom for the day, when he glanced at the calendar and noted the date. It would be one year tomorrow that he had found Riley on the side of the road.

Everything appeared to be back to "normal." Rechecks of his earlier research had turned up nothing out of order. Some people later came forward with sightings of doppelgangers and unusual experiences that had taken place in the period before Riley was sent back, but as Dr. Garson had predicted, they were quickly dismissed and ignored by mainstream media and the public.

Detective Gillespie had received his promotion and kept a safe distance from any reminder of that night—including Kip. And Kip's paranoia about black budget henchmen around every corner had eased as he got his life back on track.

One thing for certain, he would never view solar storms in the same way. And he doubted he would ever forgive the universe for so rudely thrusting him into the center of its paradoxes and conundrums. He didn't share Dr. Garson's excitement at being able to "boldly go where no one man has gone before." On the plus side, he had met Ericka Porter and had managed to convince her that he was a good guy.

"Stevens, Ted wants you to go to Philadelphia," said the assistant editor, dropping a folder of background material on Kip's desk.

Kip was startled from his musings. "Philadelphia? Why?"

"It's science week. The city is hosting a symposium with some astronauts and NASA scientists at the convention center. Ted wants you to tie it in with that program the university puts on every year to encourage high school students to go into science. Your press pass is in the folder."

Kip heaved a sigh of annoyance. "Why me? I had plans this weekend."

"Why not you? You seem to be into this scientific stuff nowadays. Look at the bright side. You get to visit your old stomping grounds again. Don't put anyone to sleep. Keep the article light. It's supposed to be inspirational."

* * * * *

Kip got off the train in Philadelphia and heard his name called.

He stopped and turned. "Mrs. Thurston," he greeted in surprise. "We meet again."

She smiled. "So we do. What brings you here?"

"I've been assigned to cover the science symposium tomorrow for the newspaper," replied Kip. "And you?"

"I'm here to help the police department with a case. Mr. Stevens, I've been wondering what became of your mystery man."

Kip hesitated, pondering how much to say. "He-uh-recovered from his amnesia and returned home," he answered. "You were right about the Slaterville tip, by the way."

Mrs. Thurston smiled. "You can thank my great grandmother," she replied. "The information came from her…. Well, it was nice to see you, Mr. Stevens. Have a good day."

As Kip watched her walk away, the psychic mentioned in Julia Trowbridge's diary suddenly leaped to mind, and he was struck by a thought. Mrs. Thurston's great grandmother couldn't be…or could she? Intrigued by the idea, Kip went on to his hotel.

The symposium room at the convention center the next day was filled to capacity. As Kip listened to the panel of astronauts talk about their experiences in space and the scientists discuss the future of the program, the exploration of the universe, and all its possibilities, he felt smug. *If you only knew*, he thought. When the session was opened to reporters, he identified himself and asked his questions.

At the end of the symposium, he was preparing to leave when he heard a voice comment, "Boy, they'll let anyone in here."

Kip turned to see a fellow reporter from his days at the *Philadelphia Inquirer* and grinned. "It would appear so," he quipped, looking pointedly at the older man.

"What are you doing here, Stevens?"

"Small towns have an interest in science, too, Larry," replied Kip.

"Yeah, I heard you were working for a small-town paper up in Fairfield. Waste of talent. I have it on good authority that, if you ask, the boss will give you back your old job. Come back to the office with me. I'll be the ice breaker."

"Thanks, Larry, but I'm happy where I am," said Kip.

Larry raised a brow, skeptical. "You sure about that? I never would have figured Kip Stevens for the dull life of a small town."

Kip laughed. "You would be amazed at what goes on in small towns."

"What about Jackie?" inquired the reporter, still unconvinced. "She knows she made a big mistake not supporting you when the shit hit the fan. She expected to hear from you by now. I venture to say she wants you back, too…and not just as a colleague," he added with a meaningful lift of his brow.

"I've come to realize that Jackie and I want different things," said Kip. "I've moved on, Larry."

"Should I take that to mean you have found someone else?"

Kip paused with the thought and smiled. "Yes, I would say that I have."

"Oh. Well, if you change your mind about the job, give me a call. Good to see you again, Stevens."

Larry melted into the crowd then.

Kip was heading for the door, when he was hailed by another attendee.

"Mr. Stevens."

Kip stopped and turned to see an attractive man about fifty, military—Air Force by his uniform. His gray hair was in the buzz cut style, and he had the unmistakable bearing of an officer. Kip recognized him as being one of the astronauts from the panel.

"I heard you announce your name at the Q and A," said the officer. "Are you from Fairfield?"

"I am. How can I help you?"

"I'm Colonel Rodgers."

"Yes, I know," said Kip. "Good presentation, Colonel Rodgers. Made me want to go into space myself."

"Thank you, sir." The colonel hesitated. "This may be a long shot, Mr. Stevens, but I wonder if you knew my grandfather—Charles Harrington."

Kip furrowed his brow. "I knew a Harrington, but not a Charles Harrington."

"My grandfather used his middle name in his profession, but the family called him Riley."

Kip looked at the colonel, dumbfounded, and it was a moment before he could speak. "Riley Harrington is your grandfather? How is he?"

"He passed away in 1986. Grandma Liza passed three years later."

Kip was taken aback, still having difficulty wrapping his head around the whole time-warp thing.

"Oh…yes, I suppose he would have passed by now," he said, quickly recovering himself. "I have often wondered what happened to your grandfather."

"Grandfather was a pioneer in the space program—one of those unsung heroes," replied the colonel. "He's the reason I became an astronaut."

Kip had to wonder again at the seamless interweaving strands of "coincidence."

"Colonel, how old was your grandfather when he died?" he asked, curious.

"Eighty or thereabouts. Grandfather was always a little vague about his age," replied Rodgers.

Quickly doing the math, Kip concluded that Riley had exited the 1907 wormhole with Elizabeth sometime around 1932.

The colonel chuckled. "Grandfather could figure any mathematical formula, but he couldn't seem to figure his birthdate. Grandma Liza said it was vanity."

The astronaut regarded Kip in bemusement then. "I expected to encounter someone much older than you, Mr. Stevens. You must have been a child when you met my grandfather."

Kip gave a slight nod. "I'm sorry I didn't get to see him again."

"I don't know what you did for him, but he said that when I meet Kip Stevens from Fairfield, Pennsylvania, I must thank you…that you had changed his life."

Rodgers puckered his brow. "Grandfather was always precise with his words. He distinctly said 'when' not 'if' I meet you. I thought the likelihood of running across you pretty remote, but Grandfather sounded pretty certain of it."

"Being one yourself, you must know that scientists are always figuring the chances of probability," said Kip.

The colonel nodded. "That is true, and Grandfather seemed to be uncannily good at it. If I may ask, Mr. Stevens—"

"Kip, please call me Kip."

"Kip—what did you do for Grandfather?"

Kip shrugged. "I cannot recall. It must have been so small an act."

The colonel smiled. "I have found that what may seem to be a small, inconsequential act to one person is sometimes a life changing event to another."

"It would seem so," replied Kip. He noticed the watch on the astronaut's wrist. "Was that your grandfather's watch by chance?"

"Why, yes. It isn't fancy—just a simple digital—but he valued it very much, and so, I value it as well. But how did you guess?"

Kip smiled. "Just a hunch. It's not the Apple Watch I would expect you to have." He looked at his own watch, anxious to be off before he said too much.

"I'm sorry, Colonel—"

"Please call me John."

"I would like to talk further, John, but I have to catch a train now," said Kip. He pulled out a business card from his pocket. "Please keep in touch. I may have a story to tell you some day."

The astronaut took the card. "Yes sir. I will do that." He gave Kip a quizzical look and held out his hand. "It was a pleasure to meet you, Kip. Somehow, I feel it was fated."

Kip smiled and shook the colonel's hand. "Or destined. The universe is a mystery unto itself."

On the train trip home, Kip thought about many things that, taken all together, people called life. But there was so much more to it than that, and it came to him that maybe instead of burdening him, the universe might actually have enriched him—Maddie Claymore would say for a purpose.

Kip thought his purpose done, but perhaps there was another. Dr. Garson had told the students that day at the university that much science had roots in fantasy and much truth resided in fiction. But discovery began with dialogue.

Kip reached for his laptop and began to write the first draft of a book. Black budget groups couldn't discredit facts disguised as fiction. Maybe one day, the world would be ready for the truth—and he could tell Colonel John Rodgers the real story of his grandfather and the watch.

Given that the human race requires, and has a certain criteria for 'proof,' which has been taught to us by the academic world, information can easily be suppressed by concealing that proof. It is no secret that the Department of Defense receives trillions of dollars that go unaccounted for and everything developed within the United States Air Force Space Agency remains classified...Within the past few years, proof has been emerging for a number of phenomenon that would suggest a whole other scientific world that operates separately from mainstream science.

—Arjun Walia

We have the technology to take ET home, anything you can imagine we already have the technology to do, but these technologies are locked up in black budget projects. It would take an act of God to ever get them out to benefit humanity.

—Ben Rich, Former CEO of Lockheed Skunk Works.

About the Author

Kathy Keller is the author of historical fiction, historical romance, and sci-fi time travel novels. She graduated from the American University, Washington, D.C. with a BA in journalism. A native of north central Pennsylvania, she currently resides in Leesburg, VA with her husband.

Books by Kathy Keller

The Homeward Heart
A Love too Proud
Destiny's Shadow
Millionaires' Row (co-author with A. J. Billman)
Millionaires' Row: The Legacy (co-author with A. J. Billman)
The Paradox
A Little Gentle Persuasion
Lady of the Sea

www.KathyKeller.com